HOMEGROWN

BY

TIM BOOKMAN

DORRANCE
PUBLISHING CO
EST. 1920
PITTSBURGH, PENNSYLVANIA 15238

Dorrance Publishing Co
585 Alpha Drive
Pittsburgh, PA 15238
Visit our website at www.dorrancebookstore.com

ISBN: 979-8-88925-100-2
eISBN: 979-8-88925-600-7

PROLOGUE

Dan McCarthy (Director of Homeland Security, Washington Division) arrived at his office and said hi to all his office staff. While holding his Starbucks coffee, he went immediately to his office to open his computer and sift through the latest emails while making notes. Once that was completed, he went through the pile of mail in the stack. He noticed one of the letters was handwritten. Instead of following protocol and sending the letter to security, for some reason he opened it. It had a heading on the letter that read "You Made Me." *Puzzling,* he thought. Then he read the rest.

"On May 11, 2027, at 9:00 A.M., the great country of the United States will start a journey that will put it on its knees and shake the country as it never could believe would happen. The event you will witness will be duplicated in severity, precisely thirty days apart, until the American people fully, 100%, acknowledge the suffering and abuse they have continued to inflict on all minority races living in our great country. They must also change and reverse all pollution leading to global warming. I do not expect this warning to be heeded until you have suffered. So suffer you shall. But please remember, <u>thirty days</u>. There is no need for discussion. The choice is clear. Only deeds will reverse the events that are going to unfold."

Dan chuckled. He thought, *WOW! This one really got creative! But how did this land in my inbox? These usually get intercepted before they hit my desk. I always read these being posted on the bulletin board.*

"Cindy!" Dan called out.

In came his secretary, a tall brunette in her late 40s. "Yes, sir. May I help you?"

Dan asked her to read the message and see how it made it to his desk.

"Hit 'copy' if you would, sir, and I'll ask around. This should have never made it to your desk." Cindy took the message from the copier and handed it to Inspector Marshall to find out how it made it so far.

John Marshall read the message and stated, "Wow! Good read! This will be fun! Might make the bulletin board for a whole week! It may be a record holder!"

As he passed it around, everyone chuckled as they stated the message should not have hit Dan's desk.

CHAPTER I

It was a warm summer evening in June 1996. DeShawn, a thin five-year-old boy, sat nervously awaiting his stepfather's arrival from work. This had become a nightly tradition for several months. DeShawn never knew what mood his stepfather would come home in.

Months before, his father Tim (an over-the-road truck driver) was in a wreck that totaled his big rig. He received a DUI, lost his license and thus his income. Now Tim was faced with the reality that truck driving was no longer an option. Each passing week, paying the bills was getting to the point where keeping the home he worked so hard for was being a passing fantasy. With each new job Tim tried and failed at, he grew ever more agitated at the world around him. Each passing night, DeShawn sat and waited to see what man would come through the door.

Today, Tim started a new job as a janitor at the FedEx Building in Pittsburgh. Halfway through his shift, his foreman walked up to him and started calling him an idiot. Tim had used the surface cleaner to clean the glass. Tim had had enough! Instead of correcting the issue,

Tim turned. He was shooting bullets out of his eyes! Tim looked at his boss of one day and, with not saying a word, threw the hardest punch he could muster! It was so hard that his foreman was knocked unconscious immediately! Blood spilled against the bathroom wall and over the floor.

Outside the bathroom, another janitor saw what was happening and ran in. "What did you do?" He pulled his phone out and called 911.

Within moments, EMS and police arrived. Despite Tim's pleads to not be arrested, he was sent to jail for assault and battery (a felony).

At home, 4:30 P.M. came. As every night, Jill (DeShawn's mom) walked through the door. Jill worked every day as a receptionist for a local dentist. She was a tall lady of 35 with a soft manner about her. She looked at DeShawn and asked where Tim was. DeShawn, worried about what this late arrival might mean, shrugged and told his mother he had no idea. Jill said it was odd, especially since dinner was expected to be served at 5:15 P.M. each evening. What could this mean?

At the police station, they gave Tim permission to make a phone call.

"Jill, I won't be home tonight."

Jill asked, "Why? What's wrong?"

Tim replied, "Don't you mind. I will tell you when and if I come home."

Jill hung up the phone while her mind was racing. What was this all about? This had never happened, except when he was in the wreck that destroyed their lives.

The next morning, Tim was in Municipal Court facing a felonious assault charge, a 4th-degree felony. His court-appointed lawyer instructed Tim to plead not guilty. He explained, with the passing of time there was a great chance of the charges being reduced. The arraignment went exactly that way and since Tim was a family man with only a DUI on his record, he was released on his own recognizance bond.

Trial was set for the following month.

Instead of calling anyone, Tim sat outside the courthouse thinking. Thinking about how everyone looked at him now, thinking about how in two short months he could go from a hard-working, respected individual to become one of the poor dregs on humanity looked down on by most of his friends and neighbors.

Several hours went by. Now with noon approaching, Tim decided to return to the FedEx Building to retrieve his car. With no money even for a bus ride, he was faced with a three-mile hike. Walking along the street, it appeared everyone was staring at him. This made him more and more agitated with each step he took. How could his whole life be turned upside down just by a couple of little slipups? How could the world be so judgmental? Yet look at all these people looking down their noses at him!

Back at home, Jill and DeShawn had a restless night. What could possibly be going on? What was going on with Tim? Jill decided to call off work the next day because she couldn't possibly concentrate on work. DeShawn was so nervous. What man would walk through the door tonight? Deep inside, he knew what it would bring.

Tim finally arrived back at his car, only to find his passenger rear tire was flat. Staring at his car, he knew someone did this to him. Storming to the entrance door, he was met by two security guards who appeared to have been waiting for this moment. They stopped him short of the entrance. As he approached the two men, he recognized them from the day he had applied for the job. The taller of the guards told Tim he might as well turn around and exit the property. Not only was he not welcome there but they also had the police on the phone. He would be arrested for trespassing.

Now, as his boiling point was nearing super volcano, Tim started shouting, "Who flattened my tire? How am I supposed to leave?"

The tall security guard, trying to calm the enraged man he only knew of as the man who assaulted a worker in the building, decided to diffuse the situation by helping get him off the property. "Look, bud. I will pull my truck around. I have a portable air compressor. If I do that, will you leave peacefully?"

Tim glared for a second at the security guard, then just spat out, "Yes."

The tall security guard told his partner to watch the man until he was able to pull his truck around. Minutes later, he brought the truck beside Tim's car and began airing the tire. The tire took air but he noticed that he could hear air leaking from the tire.

"You'd better get this to a gas station quickly. I can hear you have a leak."

Tim kicked the tire and got into the car. He had no plans of going to any place to fix the tire. By now, his anger was so intense that any normal plans were not happening. Tim pulled into the driveway of his home, turned off the engine and just sat there thinking.

Jill and DeShawn spent a troublesome morning wondering, thinking what could possibly have happened to make Tim not come home. Was Tim going to return home in one of his horrible moods? Did he have a medical issue? Or is it something different? Nothing but questions. The worrying was unbearable. If only he would call!!!

After like what seemed to be days but was only 1:30 in the afternoon, Jill heard the car pull into the driveway. Anxiously, Jill waited to find out anything. She peered out of the curtains to see Tim just sitting in the car with his head on the steering wheel, not moving, just sitting. Panicked by thinking something health related happened, she headed to the door. DeShawn asked what was happening.

"Nothing," she said anxiously. "Just go to your room until I see what is happening."

Outside, Tim sat in his car. He reached for the glovebox and took out the .38 he carried in the semi for protection and set it on his lap. After a few seconds, he checked the cylinder.

"Yep, all loaded."

The first thought he pondered was simply putting the gun to his head and ending it all. But no! He didn't because all of this… it was THEM! The rest of the world caused this! He just sat there, head resting on the steering wheel.

Jill came rushing out while DeShawn peered from the upstairs window. "Are you okay?" Jill asked Tim.

He just sat, not looking up.

Jill started to panic. She knocked on the window. "Are you okay?"

Suddenly, Tim glared up. The look coming from Tim made Jill shudder to her core! Tim had the look of a man possessed! Eyes that, by looks alone, could kill!

He violently pushed the door open. "What the fuck do you want? Can't you leave me alone? Can't I have one fucking moment to myself?!!!"

Jill, now in total panic, exclaimed, "I was worried! What is wrong? Where were you all night? I was scared!" She had never, ever seen Tim in this light. She turned and said, "You can sit out here again tonight for all I care."

Tim snapped! Now out of the car, he reached out as Jill turned her back. Then, with all his strength, he grabbed her by the back of the hair and yanked her to the ground! Jill was screaming at Tim to quit! But it was way past that point!

DeShawn was watching all this unfold and started pounding on the window and yelling, "Stop! Stop! Don't touch my mother!" But it was all in vain.

Tim was now repeatedly kicking Jill, raising her off the ground with every kick.

Mrs. Cline heard it all and came running out of the house. "Stop! Stop! I'm calling the police!"

An older black man in a beat-up Ford pickup stopped in the street and watched Mrs. Cline run back into the house to call the police.

By this time, Tim had grabbed Jill by the hair, dragged her to the house, picked her up and threw her into the door, busting it open.

DeShawn was running down the stairs, screaming at Tim, "Leave my mom alone! I'll kill you! Don't hurt my mom!!!"

Jill was scrambling, trying desperately to get up. In vain, she bit Tim's arm, clamping down so violently she bit a chunk of flesh off. For one second, Tim quit striking her and jerked back, falling into the night table and then to the floor. As he lunged back at Jill, the pistol in his pocket fell to the floor. DeShawn ran at Tim, screaming and grabbing at his leg. Tim kicked him off violently and then kicked him in the head, sending DeShawn flying. Now free, Tim grabbed the broken leg of the night table and, with all his might, swung the leg into Jill's skull. She lay lifeless.

Tim stared at her for a second and then turned to take his fury out on DeShawn. When he spun around, there stood DeShawn, holding the pistol, pointing it right at Tim. Tim threw the leg of the chair at DeShawn, right after he heard a thunderous BANG!!!

CHAPTER II

DeShawn ran to his mother, now lifeless and lying in a growing pool of blood. DeShawn cried uncontrollably as the sounds of sirens were growing increasingly louder. Outside, a growing group of people started gathering, trying to get a glimpse of what happened. Two police cars pulled into the driveway, immediately instructing bystanders to back up. Four patrolmen gathered to discuss strategy while speaking to Mrs. Cline. Finally, two more police cars pulled up to the house. Sergeant Mark McGuire first walked up to the officers who arrived on the scene first. The other officers briefed the sergeant.

Minutes later, with pistols drawn, a group of six officers approached the house. Coming to the open door, they started to witness the bloody scene. They saw broken furniture and some blood splatters. Cautiously, they peered inside. Mark peered around the corner and saw Tim's lifeless body. At first glance, he saw a bullet wound in the center of his chest. He spun his gun around the room until he saw DeShawn, crying uncontrollably, lying on his mother around a large pool of blood.

Mark gasped while wondering what happened. He told the other officers, "Call Crime Scene! Back out and don't let anyone else in until they arrive! Call Child Protective Services! We need help!"

Mark gently approached DeShawn. He looked so small. He could not fathom what could have happened.

"Son, are you alright?"

DeShawn clung to his mother with all his might.

"What your name?"

No answer.

Mark knelt down and put his hand on DeShawn's shoulder. "Let's go outside, son."

DeShawn, not wanting to go, just wept and clung to his mother. Mark put his other hand around DeShawn and firmly but gently took the crying boy outside.

Once they were outside, there stood a tall woman that appeared to be in her mid-30s with a gentle appearance.

Mark asked, "Are you with Child Protection?"

The woman replied, "Yes, I'm Karen. What seems to be going on?"

Mark went over what he saw inside and told Karen the boy would be in need of some serious help.

Karen approached DeShawn and said, "Honey, my name is Karen. Would you tell me your name?"

DeShawn stood there with tears still streaming, visibly beside himself.

Karen reached down and gave him a firm hug. "Honey, I'm here to help you. Can you tell me if there's someone I can call? Do you know any phone numbers? Do you have grandparents close?"

DeShawn just shrugged, not wanting to do anything now but to go back to his mother and gazing into the house.

Karen said, "No, honey. We need to let the policemen take care of all that."

Karen took time to ask a patrolman if he could provide the names of the people inside and to also ask the neighbors if anyone knew of any relatives. She told the officer she needed to get DeShawn away from the scene, as he clearly had been through enough.

The fire department had just pulled up. Out came several EMTs but the police instructed them to stay outside until they processed the scene.

Mark told them that clearly there was no hurry for help. There was nothing they could do, only recovery. "Maybe you can assist the other patrolmen in talking to the neighbors. There must be a long history here. This type of thing doesn't just happen. Let's start piecing this together."

Back inside, Mark barked out, "We need every inch of this photographed! Be careful! Do not disturb anything!"

As he carefully surveyed the room, he tried to form a picture in his head. The front door broke the scuffle. It must have started outside, which was confirmed by the officer who was interviewing Mrs. Cline. Next, he saw the broken table. Everything in the room was thrown about and had blood splatters on it. Jill's lifeless body lay across the room with severe trauma to her head. Tim's body was midway into the room, lying perpendicular to Jill's body. He was on his back with what appeared to be a gunshot wound through the center of his chest. There was a gun about five feet before the staircase leading upstairs. It looked to be a .38. Just lying on the floor. None of this appeared to be right.

Mark spent a few more minutes just looking around the room. Then he went back outside and spoke to the first officers on the scene. "Did anyone go inside? Did you or anyone else see any other person?"

The officers assured Mark that they were the first inside and no one had witnessed anyone else involved with the family. He looked at Mark's puzzled expression and asked him what was wrong.

Mark said, "Nothing. Just domestic violence."

The officer could tell by Mark's expression and the tone of his voice that was not the case.

Mark went back inside to talk to the crime scene investigators. The coroner had also arrived. Mark asked Dan (the head investigator) if, at first glance, he thought it would be just an unfortunate case of domestic violence. Dan looked around and said he would need more time. Mark told him to look at where the gun lay and then told him to notice how the bodies were in relationship to the gun.

"How would the mother have pulled the trigger, then throw the gun to that location? She couldn't have, the way I see it. Someone else would have had to shoot the father. But who? Could that small boy have possibly shot the father? Never have I seen a child that small be able to pull the trigger of a gun."

Dan said, "Yes, but what state of mind do you think he was in, watching his mom being beaten to death?"

They decided to wait for more evidence.

Karen now faced the facts that surrounded poor DeShawn. According to the neighbors, DeShawn's parents kept to themselves. They knew Tim was an over-the-road trucker who suddenly just quit. No more over-the-road jobs. He just seemed to work whatever he could find. Mrs. Cline knew Jill was a stay-at-home mother but had gone to work as a receptionist. But after she started the job, she changed. Never pausing to chat. She became short and distant. DeShawn, who up until last year could usually be seen scampering around the yard, this year the boy was seldom seen. He appeared to always be sullen, never the rambunctious child again. But no one knew of any relatives.

Karen started researching the records of the family. With Jill, she found no siblings. Her parents were killed by a drunk driver ten years ago.

She had a previous marriage to DeShawn's father. He was sent to prison four and one-half years ago on a murder charge. DeShawn probably never even met or had any contact with him. Tim came from a hardworking middle-class family. But when Tim married an Afro-American woman, his father disowned him and never spoke or called Tim again. So now, faced with no family, what was to become of DeShawn?

Days passed and Mark started to see the evidence come through. Now the picture was forming of what happened that terrible day. He learned of Tim's DUI that would send their life into a spiral. He learned of the numerous jobs Tim had since the time right up to his arrest the day before the murder. But by far the most troubling evidence was DeShawn's fingerprints were all over the gun and gun residue was found on DeShawn's hand. How was all of this to play out? Was it even possible to charge a boy that young with murder? Given the appearance of the house, it had to be self-defense. It just had to be!

Karen struggled with DeShawn. She didn't even want to think about putting that small boy into a detention center. So she decided foster care was where he should go. DeShawn was accepted by Bonnie and Joe Blake. They had a modest home in a middle-class neighborhood. They had no children. Joe (a construction worker) went to work and came home every day like clockwork. Bonnie (a heavyset lady in her 30s) was pleasant and treated DeShawn with kindness. She would take him to the park and get ice cream. The Blakes didn't seem to mind the fact that DeShawn was Afro-American. That was never discussed. So at least for now, DeShawn's mind could be off his mother. At least during the day. But at nighttime, the horror came back. Visions flashed through his mind.

Five days after the gruesome murder, Mark sat in District Attorney Paul Roberts' office. On the desk in front of Paul sat a pile of photos and a stack of paper.

Paul rose as Mark took a seat. "This is great," Paul said to Mark. "Everything here points to DeShawn pulling the trigger. But without talking to the boy, we cannot rule self-defense. There's no way it's anything but self-defense. I'm sorry to say this to you but we are going to need to bring him into my office so this can be sorted out."

Mark hung his head and said, "There's no other way? That poor boy witnessed all that violence and the murder of his mother! You really want this to happen?"

Paul stated there was no other way. It had to be finalized.

Karen pulled into the Blake's driveway, walked to the door and knocked.

Bonnie came to the door and asked Karen, "What's going on? De-Shawn is fine."

Karen hung her head and then said she was there to take DeShawn to the police station.

"What on earth for?" Bonnie asked.

Karen said that now that he had had time, the police would like to clear a few minor issues and close the case.

Karen pulled into the police station. She told DeShawn it was okay, that he did nothing. The police just needed to ask a few questions. But DeShawn's mind was racing. Was he going to jail? Did they know he shot Tim? It was an accident! He didn't even know how the gun fired!

They approached the office of Paul Roberts and Karen knocked on the door. They were greeted at the door by Mark.

"Well, hi, DeShawn. Why don't you come in and take a seat? Don't be worried. We are not asking anything, just questions."

DeShawn, scared out of his mind, looked around and just sank into the chair in front of Paul Roberts. Paul looked into the eyes of the small, visibly frightened boy.

"DeShawn," Paul spoke, "we know how this must be. The most

frightening thing you or anyone could imagine. I'm just going to ask you a few questions. Okay?"

DeShawn shrugged his shoulders while staring at the floor. His mind racing, he just looked down staring at the carpet under his feet.

Paul told Mark, "Why don't you take point in the questions?"

Mark started, "DeShawn, let me tell you what we know and what we don't. We know your stepfather came home agitated. He was arrested for assault the day before. We know he was brutally assaulting your mother outside your home. Then he shoved your mother through the front door. But beyond that, we just pieced the evidence together. The evidence points to the scuffle continuing in the house and your stepfather brutally hitting your mother. But DeShawn, where did the gun come from? We know you pulled the trigger. But how? How do you even know how to use a gun? Please, son. Help us fill in the blanks."

DeShawn shrugged his shoulder. He was sobbing with his hands over his face. Paul brought in Karen, hoping this might calm DeShawn.

Karen pulled up a chair beside DeShawn and gently put a hand on his leg. Speaking softly, she told DeShawn, "Please help us, DeShawn. Just tell how the gun went off. Please!"

DeShawn raised his head. This time, the tiny boy had a defiant air to his mannerisms. "I didn't know the gun would do that. I've only seen them on TV. I didn't mean to do that." Mark started to tell DeShawn it was okay but DeShawn broke in. He blurted out, "But I'm not sorry! He hurt my mom! He hurt her bad and he was going to hurt me next! It's the same every time! He's mean, mean, mean!!!"

There was a moment of silence. Then Paul spoke up, telling Mark and Karen that he believed nothing more was to be accomplished here.

Karen rose and guided DeShawn to the door. She turned and asked the two men, "So, is it over?"

Mark shook his head yes and motioned her to take DeShawn out.

As they walked to the car, Karen asked DeShawn if he was hungry. DeShawn shook his head no. So Karen drove him back to the Blakes'.

Pulling into the driveway, Karen saw Bonnie peer out the window. Bonnie met them at the door and asked Karen why the police would bring this small boy in for questioning. Karen explained to Bonnie that the police figured out DeShawn was the one who pulled the trigger but clearly it was a self-defense action.

Bonnie gasped, "This small boy? How?"

Karen told her that even DeShawn didn't know how it happened.

Bonnie took a hold of DeShawn in a bear hug and exclaimed, "You poor boy! How awful can this be?"

Bonnie let DeShawn go off to gather his thoughts while pondering her own. *This poor, poor child! How can this happen?*

Joe returned home from work two hours later, right on time. Bonnie gave him a concerned look. She told Joe they needed to talk.

Joe calmly looked at her and asked, "Something wrong?"

She went on to explain what Karen had told her.

Joe rose, hand on his chin. "Why didn't Karen say this up front? I don't like this at all! Get Karen on the phone! I want to understand this!"

When Bonnie got Karen to answer, she handed the phone to Joe. She heard Joe: "Why didn't you tell us this beforehand? Well, yes! That changes everything! I can't have this!!! I will not have a murderer under my roof!"

Bonnie picked up another phone and heard Karen exclaim, "He's just a tiny boy! It had to be an accident!"

Joe, agitated, exclaimed that it wasn't explained to him in the beginning.

DeShawn heard Joe's complaints and just sat in his room.

Karen explained to Joe that they did not know any of this until all the evidence was in, but DeShawn was a sweet boy that was caught up by domestic violence. "Surely you understand that?" Karen asked Joe.

Joe fired back, "I will not have a murderer, by any circumstance, under my roof! You get here and get here fast! I want him out!"

Bonnie blurted out, "Joe, please! Listen! He's just a tiny boy! Please understand!"

Joe said, "No! What I said is the way it's going to be! Get your ass here! Now! And get him the hell out of here!"

Joe was so loud now that DeShawn had heard all of the end of the conversation. What was he going to do? What would change things so fast? He could hear someone coming up the stairs. Bonnie appeared at his door. With tears streaming down her face, she stretched out her arms to hug DeShawn.

Karen pulled into the driveway a short time later and was met at the door by Joe. Bonnie was coming down the stairs with DeShawn, both sobbing. Joe turned and only said to leave. Karen gathered DeShawn and left the house. DeShawn turned to see Bonnie running up the stairs.

CHAPTER III

DeShawn, now eleven, had grown into a tall 5'7" frame. No longer tiny and thin but he had a mature look for a boy that age. By now, De-Shawn had lived in seven separate foster homes. There's never even been a nibble at adoption. Just bouncing around foster parents. DeShawn was never fully accepted into families either because of his past or his withdrawn attitude. He was always distant. Always reading books. Always. And not books normal for eleven-year-olds. Books on science. Odd, very odd for a boy his age. Bouncing from household to household also caused him to go to five new schools over that timeframe. Never staying put, he never developed deep friendships. He endured the challenges of new classmates. The name-calling was the worst. Because of his tall stature, he was always challenged. By third grade, he stopped being a "sheep" and started fighting back. This became troubling to school officials as well as to the foster parents who were summoned to school on way-too-frequent occasions. But after, DeShawn would withdraw to his books, always reading, always looking for the next thing he didn't understand.

On the third week of his fifth grade in school, DeShawn got dressed quickly and went downstairs for breakfast. His new foster parents, Tom and Jenny Brooks, sat at the table.

Tom greeted DeShawn, "Good morning! Sit down. A good breakfast sets the tone for the day!!"

DeShawn didn't know they were eating fruit for breakfast.

At school, DeShawn walked through the hallway. This morning, he was receiving his normal looks. This was a predominately white school in a very conservative neighborhood. Walking toward DeShawn were three boys who were the main cause of problems at the new school. Mark, the tallest of the three, was the instigator but the other two (Bob and John) were the ones who started the trouble. This day, it was Mark's turn.

DeShawn kept walking as the three approached. They veered in his direction and bumped hard into DeShawn, knocking him into a row of lockers. DeShawn ignored the brush and kept walking.

Mark called after him, "What's the matter, nigger? Too big of a pussy? Go on! Run! Run away!"

DeShawn turned his head and just glared at Mark. This just agitated the three. Then they went on their way, waving their arms as to say, "Can you believe that guy?"

Lunch in the cafeteria was always an adventure. DeShawn always sat by himself, as far away from everyone else as possible. He always sat reading a new book. Learning was his only escape in life. Immersed deeply in his book, DeShawn never noticed Mark coming up quickly behind him. As Mark got close, he swung his fist, hitting DeShawn hard in the left ear. DeShawn fell from the chair, hitting the ground hard. He really didn't know that was coming.

DeShawn jumped up in a flash, and in a fury he lunged at Mark, tackling him to the ground instantly and striking his face repeatedly. Teachers and the school resource officer came running. The resource officer knocked DeShawn off Mark and then jumped on top of DeShawn to restrain him. Mark rose to his feet, now bloodied and a bad cut on his lip.

"Take them to the office! Now!!!"

The two boys sat outside Principal Hayes' office, with the resource officer sitting between the two. They sat there until their parents arrived. Mark's parents were the first to arrive. They had the air of money about them (well dressed and obviously had a professional job, certainly not a construction worker). Principal Hayes called Mark's parents into his office. After ten minutes of explaining the situation, they called for Mark to come in. Principal Hayes asked Mark for his side of the story. Mark sat there and then said he was just walking by DeShawn and merely said, "Nice book." DeShawn jumped him for no reason.

Mark's mother, now wiping blood from his face, told the principal, "You better do something about that boy. Rumor has it that he's pretty strange."

Principal Hayes told Mark that it was his opinion that there were usually two sides to a story and that he would wait for the other side.

Outside, Tom came into the outer office. "What's going on, DeShawn?"

DeShawn told him, "Just a fight."

"DeShawn," Tom said, "you know you can't tolerate another strike against you. You are smarter than that! Hell! How can you ace all of your subjects with so little effort, yet you can't ever avoid a fight or choose not to do so? I don't get it."

Mark and his parents, coming out of Principal Hayes' office, heard the principal call out for DeShawn to bring his parents in. Tom and DeShawn both rose and entered the office.

Mr. Hayes looked at DeShawn and told him, "I thought I already saw you once this year. Let's hear your side of this one."

DeShawn told Principal Hayes how he was sitting completely away from everyone, trying to avoid any contact, and Mark hit him when he had his back to him. "They always come after me. Even this morning. First thing. I did nothing back."

Principal Hayes asked, "This is not the first time?"

DeShawn told him, "Yes, Mark's friends, they are all after me."

Principal Hayes told Tom and DeShawn to wait in the outer office until he spoke with the resource officer.

The officer had little to offer. According to him, he merely reacted to the fight, nothing before that.

Principal Hayes called everyone into the office. He rose and began speaking. "I couldn't have gotten two polar-opposite stories, exactly opposite, actually. Mark, I don't fully believe either of you two but your records speak for themselves. Mark, you have been in no trouble so I feel you will have two weeks' detention plus one week of Saturday School. You and your parents can leave."

After they left, he addressed DeShawn.

"DeShawn, this is the second time in a span of three weeks that we have spoken. I can't have that. I'm suspending you for one week. And if I hear a peep from you the rest of the year, I will suspend you permanently! We are done here."

Tom and DeShawn left the office without saying a word. They never spoke until they were in the car headed back to the Brooks' house.

Tom looked at DeShawn and said he understood being an Afro-American and at the same time also a new student. "You have to be aware of all that." He looked at DeShawn. "You know, you're running out of options."

DeShawn fired back, "I didn't do nothing! I avoided those three boys this morning! They bumped me into the lockers! I did nothing! But getting hit to the side of my head while I wasn't looking…. No! Never! That bunch has called me names for three weeks solid! Let me see you sit and take that crap for three weeks solid!"

Tom looked at DeShawn. "Son, you must find a way. It's you that will pay the price."

DeShawn asked why it was always he who paid the price. "I leave everyone alone but they start it and I pay the price! And every time it's the little rich white boys!"

Tom broke in, "DeShawn, you know how I feel about that. Me and Jenny believe everyone is the same. We don't see the color of skin. We have the same skin color. Why don't you try a little harder to fit in?"

Now back home, DeShawn went upstairs. This afforded Tom and Jenny a chance to talk.

Jenny told Tom, "You know, we have to call Karen. She told us if there are any issues, we must call. I really feel this is an issue."

"That stinks," Tom said. "You and I both know DeShawn was probably victimized here. That other boy's story made no sense. You saw the way his parents looked. They even smelled of money. Well, let's get this over with."

Jenny called Karen. When Karen answered, Jenny explained everything.

Karen listened intently and then, with a heavy sigh, exclaimed, "Let me look at my schedule. I'll need to pay a visit."

DeShawn sat upstairs reading a new book. It was on infrastructure and how the United States evolved into the modern world. The book was titled *The Critical Urban Infrastructure Handbook.* Who knew why this intrigued DeShawn, but he was reading intently, letting the world slip by.

Karen called Jenny back and they decided that she would visit DeShawn the next morning at 9 A.M. Karen told Jenny it would be best if he was not told of her impending visit.

The following morning, at 9 A.M. sharp, Jenny heard the doorbell ring. It was Karen, as promised. Jenny called upstairs to tell DeShawn someone was there to see him. DeShawn, puzzled, wondered who. Bouncing downstairs, he stopped halfway down. Oh, it was Karen. Great!

Karen sat on the couch and patted the seat as to tell DeShawn that was where she wanted him to sit. DeShawn wandered over and sat quietly. Karen asked him if he wanted to explain yesterday's events at school.

DeShawn's head sank and he said, "I suppose." He explained it as he had done the day before.

Karen broke in, "DeShawn, I told you that you must distance yourself from that stuff. The world isn't fair. I know life has dealt you the short stick, but I'm telling you this is the last stop. No more trouble anymore. Any trouble and no one will take you. Tom and Jenny told me they would be okay for a while as long as this was the last. They told me everyone raves about how smart you are and how you breeze through your schoolwork so easily. For a child who has lived your life, it is exceptionally good but let me tell you, DeShawn, the fights have to stop or the next stop for you will be a place that will not be good. So please, DeShawn! Pay strict attention to my warning! Be good! No fighting!"

The week flew by swiftly. DeShawn requested to go to the library three times. He loved it there. So many books and it was quiet. No one to bother him except so many books to choose from.

Monday morning came around. It was now time to rise and get

back to school. Deep dread crept over DeShawn. How would he be greeted? How was this going to go?

Tom greeted DeShawn at the morning breakfast table by saying, "Great new day! Fresh start! Right, buddy?"

DeShawn just said he hoped so.

They drove to the front of the school and DeShawn got out.

"Keep your head up, DeShawn! You will be alright!"

DeShawn doubted it but shook his head okay.

DeShawn walked down the hall toward his classroom, hoping not to see Mark's gang (at least for one day). Please! *So far so good,* he thought. He made it. Now cruise control until lunch.

The lunch bell rang and he went to the lunchroom. He went through the line and looked for the most secluded spot he could find. Off in the far corner, he found just a few people not in the "in crowd." He walked over and sat down and opened his book, not looking up. After he finished his lunch, he afforded himself a glance around the lunchroom. Then he spied Mark sitting with his buddies, all of them laughing and occasionally slapping the table but not looking his way. Good! He gathered his tray, cleaned it off and hurried back to his classroom.

Success! I made it!

The remainder of the day went the same way. When the bell rang sounding the end of the day, DeShawn hurried, hoping he could just get through one day. Walking outside, he found Jenny sitting in the car waiting to pick him up. He looked over his right shoulder to see Mark's clan looking at him, laughing. Mark made a fist with his right hand and struck the palm of his left hand. Then he pointed at DeShawn, turned back around and walked to his car. He told Jenny it was not over, that the boys were going to get him. Jenny tried to assure DeShawn that he would be alright. That he was imagining it. DeShawn just peered out the window, knowing that was not the case.

At home, Tom was anxiously waiting to know how the day went. Jenny merely told him great.

"Why? What did you expect?" Tom sighed, and they all went inside.

The following day, everything went just as it did the day before, until DeShawn stepped into the school. Today, the three were waiting for him. DeShawn ignored the three and started walking to his classroom. They followed. They were calling him names. "What's the matter, nigger boy?" They kept saying it over and over and over. Then one of them swiped at DeShawn's foot, sending him sprawling over the floor. Keeping his cool like nothing happened, he just got up and kept walking to his classroom.

They taunted, "You just wait! It's coming! We're going to get you, DeShawn!"

DeShawn arrived at his classroom. *Good! I made it! All is well!*

Lunchtime came and he surveyed the room as usual. He finished and then peered around. *Humph! All's good.* He emptied his tray and then decided to use the bathroom before returning to class.

DeShawn went to the urinal to take care of business when suddenly he heard, "What ya going to do now, nigger? No one to save ya!"

Now DeShawn turned and there was Mark in front and the other two boys at his side. They tackled DeShawn, taking him to the ground. While all three were throwing blows nonstop, DeShawn covered his head and turned to lay on his stomach. The blows kept coming. Somehow, DeShawn was able to get a good elbow in someone's jaw. Finally, he got to his knees.

"Now, let's go!"

He swung and hit Mark in his groin. Now he made it to his feet and lunged at Mark, throwing him into the sink. It sounded awful. Mark's head hit the sink and he fell silent. The other two boys stopped, allowing DeShawn to flee to his classroom. Quietly sitting in the classroom, looking at his book, listening to his teacher. He wondered, *Is it over?*

An hour passed when the teacher looked to the door leading out of the school. The resource officer was signaling through the glass in the door for the teacher to come to the hallway. Once in the hallway, the officer told him they wanted to talk to DeShawn.

The teacher went back to the door and asked DeShawn, "Will you step out here for a minute?"

All of the other students just stared.

DeShawn sank. *Well, let's see what this brings,* he thought.

He stepped into the hallway. The resource officer told him that he would need to meet and talk to him in private. DeShawn could only imagine where this was going. What happened after he left the bathroom? Those boys jumped him! He was just trying to get away!

DeShawn and the resource officer went into the waiting room outside Principal Hayes' office.

The resource officer began, "DeShawn, you hurt that boy bad."

DeShawn's heart began to pound.

"The boys said you followed them into the bathroom and attacked Mark with no provocation. He's been taken to the hospital."

DeShawn could not believe what he was hearing! "No! No! No! Those boys jumped me! I was avoiding them! I was being careful not to see them! I was just getting away!"

The resource officer told him they had three boys telling him a completely different story. Now he had a student in the hospital and his parents were screaming for answers. "DeShawn, I know this is not the first time you have been involved in this type of activity. We are going to have to file a police report, but I must tell you that it doesn't look good." Then he rose and went to fill in Principal Hayes.

Moments later, Principal Hayes came out and told DeShawn that his foster parents were coming to pick him up. He was suspended for the semester and would only be let back in school after counseling.

Jenny arrived to find DeShawn sitting outside the office, looking like the world collapsed. She asked what was going on.

DeShawn said, "Why does it matter what I say? No one believes me. You all believe everyone in the world but me. It's been this way my whole life. White boys life, I pay the price. Go on in and talk to the principal. It's all my fault. Go on. Be one of them."

Principal Hayes went on to explain everything to Jenny. Then he told her that she faced serious challenges with "that boy."

Later at home, Jenny and Tom called Karen to explain the situation. Karen told them she would talk to her supervisor but it seemed to her that DeShawn might have reached his limits with foster care.

Karen arrived at the house later that day to speak to DeShawn. She started by telling him that she had warned him.

Looking defiant, DeShawn fired back, "I don't care! You won't listen to anything I say! None of you do!"

Karen responded, "Well, DeShawn, I am not like that. I really have no choice but to try and send you to a facility to get some help. Not for a long time. Just until we get some good results back about your behavior."

CHAPTER IV

A black van pulled into Shuman Juvenile Detention Center. Karen stepped out, followed closely by DeShawn in handcuffs.

DeShawn peered around the portico in disbelief. DeShawn thought, *Here I am. Three days after my twelfth birthday. What a life!*

Karen ushered DeShawn to the day guard, an imposing man of six feet that didn't look to be the type she would want to chat about how the day was going.

"Paperwork?" the guard asked bluntly.

Karen handed over an envelope to the guard. He opened it and read every piece of paper.

He then put his hand on DeShawn's shoulder and said, "In this room, not a sound." He then turned to Karen and told her, "I'll process him. You can leave. He's ours now."

Once his handcuffs were removed, DeShawn was told to strip. He took all of his clothes off, down to his underwear.

The guard told him, "I said strip! Then step into that room," as he pointed to his left.

Once he walked into the other room, an intimidating lady there just pointed to the shower and told him to scour every inch or they would do it for him. So in he went and tried to follow every instruction. Stepping out of the shower, he noticed a pile of clothes sitting on a plain metal bench. An orange jumpsuit, white underwear and orange flip-flops. He put them on. They were tight, too small for him, but he never spoke a word, too frightened by the thought of what was the rest of the place was like.

After what seemed like hours but was only minutes, another guard walked in. This guard looked younger and not as mean looking, but this was only a guess. "Stand up," he told DeShawn as he reached out and put a set of handcuffs back on with ankle bracelets. "You will be treated fine as long as all of the rules are followed. Step out of line or if you don't listen, there will be hell to pay."

DeShawn listened intently as a long list of rules were read. They basically told him that he would have no privileges except what the guards gave him.

DeShawn was led down a long hallway to a large room with a TV, numerous tables (some for games, some just for sitting along the walls). There were five doors coming into the room with signs posted "Door 1-5." DeShawn was given a pillow, white sheets and a plain gray blanket. Then he was led to Door 3. Walking into the room, there were two rows of bunkbeds, stacked two high. He looked and thought there were a hundred beds but in fact, there were only sixty. Still a lot.

The guard told DeShawn to sit at the table directly in front of him until the day guard for that dorm arrived. "Mr. Dillard will be here shortly. The group will be coming back from day exercises in a few minutes."

Sitting in this large room, he peered around, looking at all the orderly made beds each with a footlocker at the foot of the bed. He could not think it was like this all of the time. Then down the hallway, he could hear the sounds of footsteps. They were in sequence. All the steps were marching in time. Then the door opened. In front was a big, robust white man leading a group of kids DeShawn's age in perfect step. As they came into the room, they formed two perfect rows. Once all were in line, they all stomped on the floor once, all at the same time. Then fell into complete silence.

Then, the man leading them (DeShawn assumed was Mr. Dillard) said, "Afternoon school starts in five minutes! Get your books and head to your assigned classrooms! No bullshit! Dismissed!"

Mr. Dillard walked to DeShawn and sat down across from him. He told DeShawn that he really didn't care about his story or what got him there. It only mattered what he did from this point on. He told De-Shawn that bunk 27 was his and for him to look at the other bunks. His bunk was never to look different. He would also be given one attempt to march in step before punishment would happen. Beds were for sleeping and he was not to touch it for any other purpose. They showered together, ate together, walked together and played together as one. Any step out of line would mean punishment.

"Do you understand what was just said to you?"

DeShawn shook his head yes.

"Now when the rest leave, you stay behind. Put your bedding on in the proper way and then the counselor will come and give you an assessment for proper school placement. Do not let him give me a bad report! Bad reports will not go as you think! They are met with no discussion!"

DeShawn peered at all the beds and how they were made. How the blanket was tucked in, how the pillow was placed. He looked at every detail before he went to find bunk 27. It was on the left row of beds from the entrance door, bottom bunk, three beds from the back of the room.

Nice, he thought, *the bottom bunk and back of the room. This might work.*

He went into recreating what the other bunks looked like. As he completed the task, into the room came an older white lady with glasses, heavyset but not fat. Her gray hair was cut short but looked good on her.

She spoke to DeShawn. "I see your name is DeShawn and you're twelve years old. Your records reflect you were to finish fifth grade in a few weeks. I must say all A's are nice but not typical for most I see here. Classes here are not what you are used to. We spend all day in school. Your grade is determined by how fast you progress. So for now, you will be placed starting in level sixth grade. Do you understand?"

DeShawn shook his head yes.

"Okay. Now let's show you the facility. Then I need you to join the rest of the dorm mates."

She took DeShawn throughout the facility, the day room, outdoor rec yard, classrooms, etc. But when they came past a room that said "Detention RMS 1-10," she stopped.

She then told DeShawn, "You need to go in there. See what happens when you get out of hand."

DeShawn went into the room numbered 8. He thought, *If this is not a jail cell, I don't know what is.*

The heavy door had a small window in it and a window on the other side with three small slats to look out. It had a bed of poured concrete and a toilet with a sink together, built into a block wall.

She told him, "Look around, because if you screw up you'll make this your home."

Then they went to the laundry area, where DeShawn was given a fresh jumpsuit. This one had a label printed with "3/27."

"This is your new name. Remember it. 'DeShawn' will not exist until you are released. You will only be called '3/27' from us. It's time to join dorm group."

A whistle blew and DeShawn watched as five lines quickly formed. Each group appeared to be a separate age group, his being next to the youngest. There was a group of younger kids. It seemed impossible that there were kids there younger than DeShawn, but there were a group of at least thirty boys under twelve years old.

DeShawn went to the line forming behind Mr. Dillard. He went to the end of the line and stood there like the other boys. The other lines started marching. Mr. Dillard stood still. DeShawn wondered what was going on. Mr. Dillard left the front of the line and started walking back through the boys.

As he approached DeShawn, he poked DeShawn's nametag and said, "See your name, stupid? Does 27 look like it belongs behind 49?" Then he grabbed DeShawn by the arm and roughly took him up the line. "No, 27 belongs between 26 and 28! Pay attention or ask!!! Strike one! You get it?"

DeShawn could feel a hot sensation, partly anger and partly fear. All he could think was to watch the feet in front of him. Mr. Dillard returned to the front of the line and started walking. DeShawn kept looking down, trying to keep in step. He was so intent on watching the boy's footsteps in front of him. He did not see Mr. Dillard raise his hand. All the boys stopped but DeShawn didn't. He ran into the boy in front, causing him to bump the next boy.

Mr. Dillard spun around. "This is my line! I guess we will learn to walk like a unit. So let's try this again and again!"

They did for the next two hours, right through dinner.

When they finally halted, Mr. Dillard turned and told them, "Well, look there! We missed dinner! Wow! I guess breakfast will really taste good!" Then he turned and walked the group to their dorm.

Mr. Dillard immediately ordered the group to start showers in groups of ten. So this meant DeShawn had a while to scope what dorm life would be like. His bunk was surrounded by one other black kid, one Latin kid and two white boys, not talking, just reading or trying to nap. The boy to DeShawn's left (number 26) was also a black kid of DeShawn's age.

DeShawn said, "Hi. I'm DeShawn. What's this place like?"

The other boy told DeShawn, "Don't let anyone here you telling your name. Say '3/27.' Be safe."

DeShawn said, "I'm sorry about the march. I didn't mean to cause that."

The boy (3/26) replied, "Mr. Dillard does that every time a new black kid comes in. Just watch yourself."

DeShawn asked why.

Number 3/26 replied, "Just listen is all. I'm saying you're black. It's always our fault."

The second group went to the shower. DeShawn just lay there feeling total fear and confusion. Eventually, his turn to shower came. The area was all white tile with no partitions, completely open. DeShawn had never been in a room with other people completely naked. He could almost hear his teeth chattering from fear. He told himself to suck it up. That he could do it and to just not make a scene. He undressed and then went to the first available shower head and lathered up.

As he was finishing, a tall redheaded boy walked up behind him and said softly, "Watch yourself, nigger. This won't be fun."

DeShawn tried not to panic. He thought, *Just finish. Just finish.*

After everyone completed showers in the dorm, the night guard came in and said, "Lights out!" Then he turned and went out the door opposite the entrance.

DeShawn could see him through the glass. Even though the lights were turned off, you could see really well. After what seemed to be an eternity of thinking about what this new world would bring, sleep finally came.

Suddenly, he was awoken by a pillow pressed against his face. He could feel punch after punch while he was struggling to breathe. Suddenly it stopped and he heard, "Nigger! Watch your step! You are going to be here a long time! Get used to it!" Then they left.

The only glimpse of anyone he saw was the tallest boy with red hear. DeShawn lay there holding his ribs and sobbing slightly so no one could hear him crying.

Mr. Dillard stepped in and yelled, "Fifteen minutes until breakfast! Bed inspection in ten!"

DeShawn got up and felt the sharp pains of the night before but he put that behind. He must be perfect today, he thought. Struggling through the pain, he got in line by ten minutes, as Mr. Dillard inspected the beds. DeShawn peered around the room. Who were all the boys that attacked him? He saw two redheaded boys but had no way of knowing who.

They marched to breakfast. They sat in numerical order for breakfast. They were served clumpy oats with a white powdered doughnut. *Better get used to it,* he thought as they ate.

A guard walked around and handed the group any new assignments. He came to DeShawn and said, "3/27! Report to classroom 5 for sixth-grade classes." Then he left.

No talking was allowed in the lunchroom. DeShawn wondered where the room was.

After exactly fifteen minutes, Mr. Dillard stood and yelled, "Clean trays and form line, now!"

Each did as instructed. Leading them down the corridor, he called out each classroom they passed and said, "Enter." Each time, several would enter the classroom. Finally, he said the sixth-grade classroom and the bulk of the boys went into the room, leaving Mr. Dillard.

The classrooms were just small desks looking forward. The entry door was heavy with a small window. The teacher for the class came in and very calmly explained the day's lesson plan. It was going to be math in the morning, followed by history in the afternoon. She lectured for an hour on basic math and then handed out worksheets that were supposed to take two hours to complete. She said if anyone completed early, they would be able to go into the library. They started on the sheets.

DeShawn looked at it and thought, *Is this a joke? It's all baby work. This was easy two years ago!* He completed it within a half an hour.

Turning in the paper, the teacher looked at DeShawn and said, "All questions need answered."

DeShawn replied, "I did. Look at it."

The teacher turned the pages and said, "Why, yes. I guess so. You may go ahead and read in the library."

After DeShawn was there an hour, in walked Mr. Dillard. He sat down and asked DeShawn if he had been good in school. DeShawn told him he guessed so, that no one ever asked him that. He usually read about stuff by himself. Teachers never paid attention to him. Mr. Dillard told DeShawn he might have to make other arrangements. That the school might not be suited for him.

Over the next few days, DeShawn started getting to know a couple of the boys during their one hour of free recreation. He was settling in to a routine. Rec time was totally white on white, black with black. It was weird. School, on the other hand, was confusing. The teachers told DeShawn that he was already smarter than their twelfth-grade level at his age. So he spent his days in the library, which suited him fine. So he read and kept requesting better books.

The weekend brought boredom, lying around with nothing at all to do except for church on Sunday. He decided on a non-denominational Protestant church. But, the first time he went, he discovered he was the only black person there. So the next day at free rec he asked the other black inmates where they attended. They said they attended a little mosque that the Shuman Center had set up. DeShawn knew little of it but he would be able to go somewhere away from all the white boys.

Kaleb (number 3/12) told him the Iman's name was Omar Kalier. "He's a nice man and he really does try to help us."

DeShawn made up his mind that this Sunday was going to be his first trip to a mosque.

The week went by quickly for DeShawn. Classes were easy and even studying at a senior level, he finished his work all in record time! His teachers couldn't believe that a child that bright would be there. That was the only time of the day that was any good. The guard picked on him constantly, often blaming him for things he couldn't have possibly have done. But as long as he could finish work early and get to the library, he could have three hours of not being 3/27.

Sunday came and he marched with the group headed to the mosque. Inside the room set aside as a mosque, they each were greeted by Iman Omar Kalier. He said hi to each one.

When he came to DeShawn, he asked, "And whom may you be?"

DeShawn answered, "3/27."

Omar said, "Child, in this place, that is not your name. Please speak the truth."

With that DeShawn told him his name. The Iman welcomed him to his mosque. DeShawn was like a fish out of water. He knew nothing of the prayers and had never read anything of the Koran. But everyone there was nice and led him through the service. As nervous as he was, he really did feel comfortable. *This may be my other happy place,* he thought!

Christmas and New Year's Day came and went, but they meant nothing to DeShawn. What did matter was the fact that he was still here. But where would he go, he thought, back to a foster home? All he was getting from the counselors was that he wasn't ready to move on. This he couldn't understand. Aside from a few shoving matches, he was content to sit back in the shadows. Don't make waves. He was becoming good friends with the Iman. Omar was impressed that DeShawn had already read the Koran and was reading other books: *Live in the Footsteps of the Prophet;* and *Lessons from the Life of Mahammed & The Study of Koran: Its History and Place in Muslim Life.* Omar was impressed. He and DeShawn would talk about it time and time again. DeShawn had decided that maybe asking Omar about what he thought he should do after this place or if he thought he would never leave. After the service Sunday, he asked the Iman to speak with him in private. Omar told De-Shawn he would make time one day in the coming week. DeShawn was excited and couldn't wait for the chance at a real one-on-one.

Wednesday morning breakfast and school went as usual. But when DeShawn was dismissed for finishing early, he was instructed to meet with Omar. So the guard took DeShawn to Omar's office. Inside, Omar told DeShawn to have a seat and then asked what was on his mind. DeShawn told him that he had been at the facility going on six months and, for the most part, had followed the rules. He had only been in trouble a few times. He just had no idea of if he was ever getting released and if he did, where would he go? The Iman told De-Shawn he would start looking into it and try to see if he could find the answers. DeShawn thanked him. The Iman rose and told DeShawn that he followed his learning of the faith and felt DeShawn's mind and spirit were really coming around. But for him to be whole, DeShawn must also develop his body. So DeShawn went outside to the waiting guard, who led him to the library.

The following week, Omar called DeShawn back to his office. He told him that he didn't have any good news. According to the Iman, the administrators at the facility had no immediate plans for him. The only order they had was to hold him indefinitely. He told DeShawn that with no one on the outside petitioning for his release, he could possibly be in for a long stay. DeShawn sunk. He rose and told Omar that none of the stuff that got him in there was his fault. Every time it was a setup. He had never done anything. It was all was staged by others.

Omar told DeShawn, "That may be true, but this might be Allah's way of testing your soul to see if your resolve could pass the test. Go back to your faith, DeShawn. Continue to strengthen your body, mind and soul."

With that, DeShawn returned to the library.

AUGUST 9, 2027

DeShawn awoke. It was his 17th birthday. He went to peer into the mirror. There stood a strong young man, six feet tall, 220 pounds and all muscle. But in this place, almost everyone was all muscle. He thought about the day ahead. He was now taking classes in his final year of college. He had made it through to getting his degree in Mechanical Engineering, a feat that took a lot of strings being pulled to even being able to take the classes, let alone being able to get accredited. But with Omar's help, it came true. Omar had DeShawn come to the mosque each day after classes to help with the lesson of the week.

Omar thought of DeShawn as possibly being an Iman of his own right one day.

So on his birthday, Omar told DeShawn something special. He told DeShawn to sit down. "I have something very special to present you. I have been speaking to a cleric in Philadelphia named Mahammed Majid. He worships at a mosque called Al-Rasdeen Islamic Center. We have spoken often about you. He is anxious to have you come live at the center until your 18th birthday, if you wish. I have cleared it with the facility. They have no need to hold you any longer."

DeShawn rose and told him, "Praise Allah! I thought this day would never come!"

CHAPTER V

It was Tuesday morning. Mr. Dillard led the group to breakfast. As they entered the dining hall, Mr. Dillard said, "3/27, report to Administration immediately following breakfast."

DeShawn was hoping big things. He could barely eat his breakfast.

After the group was led toward the classrooms, a guard was waiting at the Administration wing. He yelled, "3/27! This way!"

DeShawn was led into the warden's office. Inside, he noticed the name plaque of Warden Thompson. He was an older, large white man who appeared to have spent his life here.

"Sit down, 3/27." He peered at his paperwork and then told DeShawn, "Tomorrow, Wednesday, August 12, at 8:00 A.M., you will be released to a Mahammed Majid. He will take you to the Al-Rasdeen Islamic Center in Philadelphia, PA. You will no longer be under our guidance. I hope the lessons you have learned here will guide you through life so as to never land behind bars again. We have been harsh on you. It was on purpose. Look back on your stay here and know full well it was intended that way. Now you are dismissed. Good luck to you."

The following morning, DeShawn left the dining hall precisely at 8:00 A.M. He was met by a guard. He was led to the portal into the portico. He was given a white t-shirt, gray jacket and a gray pair of pants. DeShawn couldn't believe even dressing in clothes like these. He was taken to another room, where a man sat waiting. He was wearing a turban on his head but he was otherwise dressed in casual clothes. By his skin tone, DeShawn guessed he was of Arab descent.

The guard told DeShawn, "This is Mr. Mahammed Majid. Until your 18th birthday, he will be your legal guardian."

He asked if DeShawn agreed, which DeShawn quickly did.

Mahammed led DeShawn to a white car. By the decals on it, it was a Honda Accord. Once on the road, Mahammed told DeShawn that Omar had filled him in with DeShawn's story. He had heard how he discovered the faith and marveled at DeShawn's grasp. He also was very interested in the story of his intelligence and said that his true potential had never even been tested. He told DeShawn about Al-Rasdeen and the wonderful pursuits that they achieved. He felt DeShawn would flourish and further learn about all the wonders of the religion of Islam. He went on to tell DeShawn he also knew of how DeShawn had suffered at the hands of the infidels and that through his teachings DeShawn would be able to rise above them. He told him that the people of Islam had the ability to rise above the infidels to find their place in power.

"Now, would you like to have your first lunch outside, possibly McDonald's?"

DeShawn excitedly said, "Yes! I would very much like this!"

They didn't arrive at the center until 3 P.M. Mahammed took De-Shawn to one of the out buildings and showed him his room. Mahammed told him to spend a little time and that he would come back at 4:30 P.M. to show him around. Then they might go out and buy DeShawn some clothes. DeShawn took everything in, in amazement.

Mahammed took DeShawn downtown to go through the shops. He was showing him the styles that many were wearing.

"DeShawn," he said, "don't get caught up in the way of this nation. Look around! Homeless people, drug addicts, prostitutes, etc. This nation lost its way! Many years ago, you could walk around and feel the hatred coming from all races. You must try to stay the way of Allah. Keep your mind and body free of such trappings. If so, your life will lead you on a patch to eternal bliss."

DeShawn took this all in as he peered everywhere. Yesterday, he couldn't have imagined how busy the world was. But he was yet to understand what Mahammed meant. This was so grand to take in. It was fun to find clothes that were different than everyone else's around. He could be himself. Free at last! They had dinner at a little diner. DeShawn had two large hamburgers and fries! They tasted so good! His head was in the clouds!

After Mahammed returned him to his room, he told him not to stay up late because he must rise early for his prayers. Afterward, he would show DeShawn how he was to become useful to the center. "But remember, as you relax, what I told you about how this nation is. We will learn how it got this way later."

The next morning, DeShawn awoke to chimes telling him it was time to get ready for morning prayers. He had not performed them in such a place before. But, as he knelt beside Mahammed and the others that gathered, he really felt this was his way. Not to be huddled in pews beside a bunch of white people looking down their noses at him. He was accepted here. Truly accepted!

After the prayers, Mahammed asked DeShawn to come to his office. Once there, Mahammed went on to tell DeShawn before his release, Omar explained to him his exceptional intellect and about how DeShawn was. So Omar came to Philadelphia and visited Temple University. He showed them what DeShawn had accomplished in school and how fast he learned, about how far he rose above his environment. Two weeks later, Omar got what he wanted: a letter accepting DeShawn into Temple to get a Master's degree in Mechanical Engineering.

DeShawn could not contain himself! "Why didn't Omar tell me? Do you think I can call him? This is so great! I really need to thank him!"

Mahammed told him he could but it needed to wait until evening, as he must spend the day to understand his daily duties at the center. "But we also have a meeting with the dean at the Temple Engineering Department at noon. So let's get started."

By touring campus, DeShawn learned his duties. The one he immediately took to was cleaning the library. It was massive, with tons of books on every subject. But most were books about the Islamic religion. He was also supposed to clean the mosque after evening prayers. When Mahammed was walking DeShawn to where he would find his supplies, the Iman met them. He said "Good day" to Mahammed and asked if this was the young man he had spoken so highly of. Mahammed said it was.

"This is DeShawn. DeShawn, this is our Iman Ahmed Rahman. He is a wise and very devout leader of the center. Let's make our daily tasks joyous as to praise his leadership."

DeShawn told him he would work hard to please all the faithful to win their loyalty.

Ahmed bowed his head and said, "Praise Allah! Go with grace."

With that thought, they headed out to the meeting at Temple University.

The drive was short to the university. DeShawn thought if he had a car he could make the trek in about ten minutes. The campus was beautiful, not what he expected at all. Mahammed led DeShawn to a building that merely read "Engineering." It was mainly built out of brick but adjoined a large seven-story glass building. Mahammad told DeShawn that the building held most of the labs for engineering. Inside it was large and open with a lot of interior glass walls. He could see many students working inside. He did notice that all appeared older than him but that didn't bother him.

They entered the office of the Dean of Engineering and met Dean Moore, surprisingly a younger man. He rose briefly and asked them to be seated.

"Glad to see you again, Mahammed. We miss you around here. Are you still looking for a higher self being or are you ready to come back for work?"

Mahammed chuckled, "No, I think I'll stay the course. I have much to accomplish. This is the young man I spoke of. This is DeShawn."

DeShawn bowed his head slightly and said, "I'm honored to meet you, Dean Moore."

The dean looked DeShawn over and then told him that he was, by far, the youngest student who ever received a scholarship to get a Master's degree. "It is so impressive, almost too hard to believe, that a boy who has had the life you have had has the drive and capacity to learn the way you do. DeShawn, when I met Iman Kalief, he told me your story. You have led a very unfortunate life. I hope we can help you put all that behind you. I know Mahammed will certainly be a great role model. Omar also brought your school records and transcript of your online degree from Wright State. They were the highest test scores I have ever witnessed! And to come from a young man barely seventeen is a miracle! You are quite the prodigy, young man!"

Again, DeShawn thanked him. Then he told the dean that given the time he had through his life afforded him with the love of reading. He had never had the desire to have a lot of friends. He found most people never liked him. So it was always reading. Dean Moore told DeShawn not to waste this opportunity and to take advantage of all Temple University had to offer. He also wanted to see if this young boy would meet the potential of that Iman.

Mahammed thought he would. He told DeShawn he would be admitted the next morning and that today he would escorted around the Engineering complex. "Good luck, young man."

A young intern met them outside. He was a graduate student. "Hi. My name is Paul." He asked Mahammed, "Anything you want to see first?"

He answered, "Not me. It's him."

Paul replied, "Oh! I'm sorry! Do you want to walk through our Bachelor programs?"

Mahammed broke in, "No. He's here on a Master's scholarship."

"Wow! You're serious! Right? That's amazing! How old are you?"

DeShawn answered, "Seventeen."

Paul said, "Well, you are going to cause some talk for sure!"

As they walked to the various lecture halls and labs, DeShawn quizzed Mahammed on how the dean knew him so well. Mahammed told DeShawn that he actually went here and was in the same class as Dean Moore. He went on to explain that he was a Godard scholar and finished ahead of Dean Moore.

"Wow!" DeShawn said. "So why abandon your field? There is so much we can do to help our people and serve our faith without searching for western riches."

"Don't get caught up in this culture. Stay true to your faith. There are greater rewards than wealth," Mahammed went on and did. "Did you know Omar attended his studies here but he studied philosophy? Good student, I used to hear."

They ate a quick meal and then headed back to the center.

DeShawn asked, "When can I call Omar? I must thank him immensely."

"After evening prayers. You also have work to do. Don't disappoint me."

DeShawn called Omar after prayers. Omar was overjoyed to hear how joyful DeShawn had become in just 48 hours. He instructed De-Shawn to take great heed into the teaching of Mahammed and Calif Rahmed. They would guide him in the way of Islam.

DeShawn sunk himself into his new life: his work and studies at the center, as well as excelling in his studies. But as in the past, every time he interacted with white people bad experiences happened.

One time, he was doing a lab project in school with two others. The project involved a CNC machine and a lathe. As he approached the CNC machine, a white student said, "You might be one smart nigger, but work? You don't have that in you!"

After each of these encounters, DeShawn would visit the counselors on the third floor. But they would tell DeShawn to ignore it. He was surely the bigger man. He would also consult Mahammed. He would say, "That is the teachings of the infidels. Just learn. The day will come when they will bow to your presence. Learn from these experiences but never forget them."

The next year flew by.

AUGUST 9, 2014

Finally, DeShawn was now eighteen but what did this mean, he thought? He had no money. He had at least one-half of his schooling remaining. All these thoughts but no ideas. Was the center going to make him leave? How would he live? Fear surrounded him. He headed to the library. As he opened the door, he saw Mahammed and his friends from the mosque standing.

"Happy Birthday!" everyone yelled.

DeShawn looked around and saw a table with a punch bowl and a cake that said "Happy 18th." DeShawn had never had a birthday party before. So he took it all in. He had no idea what to do.

Once everyone sang Happy Birthday to him, they asked him to cut the cake. Everyone was very festive, not a side that DeShawn was used to seeing. He got some cake and a glass of punch. Then he took a seat by Mahammed.

"How did you put this together? I had no idea that you would even remember when my birthday would come!"

"Why would you think that?" Mahammed answered.

"You never speak of such things," DeShawn said.

"Well, you just have a good day, then! Later this evening, we will sit and talk."

DeShawn shook.

Later that evening, Mahammed told DeShawn that he deserved a little cheer. He knew how hard he worked the past year, working his way through half of his Master's degree while earning praise from the college every step of the way. And at the same time, furthering his religious teachings and duties. But he also told DeShawn that he had to leave for several months, that he was returning to Syria to meet his brothers. DeShawn, now thoroughly confused, asked Mahammed what he was supposed to do.

Mahammed laughed. "Why don't you stay here and continue your teachings? I'll never leave you stranded. We are all your family, a family in God. The people of Islam never turn their backs on each other. Have faith in the brotherhood and the brotherhood will have your back."

"Thank you, Mahammed," DeShawn said.

"Now go on and get some sleep. We have nothing but big days ahead."

Two days later, Mahammed boarded a flight to London.

For two months, DeShawn never heard from Mahammed. Then suddenly, while cleaning the mosque, Iman Calief told DeShawn that Mahammed was returning the next day. He went on to explain to De-Shawn that through the grace of Allah, Mahammed had risen to the rank of a cleric. Once he returned, he would have but six months before his permanent return to Syria.

The next day, DeShawn rode back to school and entered the library to do his cleaning and grab some time to read. Mahammed met him.

"Great to see you, DeShawn. I felt it was like a year since I have seen you! Look at how you filled out in two short months! Allah has blessed you with the brain and muscles of ten men. You will be a fine soldier of the faith. Tonight, after prayers, we will talk. I have much great news you need to hear."

DeShawn told him he could not wait. Then he went about his tasks.

Later, back at his room, DeShawn sat quietly reading when Ma-hammed entered. He told DeShawn that he met with Ayatollah Ma-hammed El Faziza, who was a great leader of the Shia Muslims battling the ways of the decrepit westerners.

"He has requested to meet you after your graduation. We have many servants around the country in the service of Allah, all who report back to El Faziza. It is he who will best figure out how we honor Allah. But that is in the future. A boy your age is hard to keep on task but, if you are who I think you are, we are okay."

The next day, it was back to normal: prayers, school, duties, prayers, home, stay, study, stay to the faith. As the weeks went on, all was good. Dean Moore summoned DeShawn to quiz him on his thesis. DeShawn told the dean that it was well on its way to being completed.

Dean Moore again challenged DeShawn on the topic. "DeShawn, the dark nature of your thesis leaves me…really quite disturbed. To discuss the fragility of our nation is debatable: 'Western Infrastructure and Its Demise.' I hope you can prove this, but I must say that I hope you can't."

The following week, DeShawn approached Mahammed. "I need a favor. I need to practice my thesis presentation. Would you be able to take time one evening to sit for an hour to listen to my thesis and defense? I will need to practice before I argue to the panel."

Mahammed said, "Of course I will. Just let me know when you're ready."

DeShawn said he still needed a couple of days to make charts and handouts to solidify his thesis.

That Friday, after prayers, DeShawn told Mahammed that he was as ready as he could be and if he had the time, they could put this behind them.

Mahammed said, "Nine o'clock? Let me meditate and I'll be ready."

Mahammed arrived and said, "You ready? I'm ready to get my socks knocked off."

DeShawn looked pale, scared out of his mind, but he mustered his faith and said, "Yes, by the will of Allah."

DeShawn mustered himself and asked Mahammed to sit on the couch. DeShawn stood up in front and began.

"Welcome. My name is DeShawn Carter. I am an eighteen-year-old man from Pittsburgh, PA. I have not led a normal life but through my diligence, I worked harder than most to rise above my surroundings to get here. The title of my thesis is 'Western Infrastructure and Its Demise.'" He handed Mahammed several handouts, including pictures of refineries, cell towers, power plants, dams and water plants. "These are all examples of where our infrastructure is developed. I am prepared to show just how vulnerable these are and how easy our western civilization has made it, not only to disrupt it but to destroy it."

DeShawn handed Mahammed more papers, each showing maps of the United States. Maps with gas lines drawn crisscrossing the United States, powerlines, fiberoptic lines. All showing intersecting and crossing.

"How did I get these? All I did was a simple Google search. I then tried to find if I could locate their exact position. So through my visits to various power plants and refineries, I learned that I could narrow it down by county, city and city block. I would simply call 811. They not only come and pinpoint the location, they will color code what piece of our infrastructure lies beneath. Most gas, telephone power and fiberoptic lines lay just two feet below the ground at best case, enclosed in about four feet of concrete. So I asked myself why this great society with such great wealth would leak all this information so unprotected and why would it put locations out for the general public. When I discovered much of this, I moved my focus from how to build more to how do we correct this and is it possible. Gentlemen, the answer is no.

Too much is in place. Too much information is out there. My hope is that this information becomes buried. Not only buried but destroyed. Thank you very much."

Mahammed looked up and asked, "Are you sure? They will not accredit this."

DeShawn said he knew that and didn't care. "I don't need their degree. I'm going to leave with you to Syria. We all know this place is destined to be destroyed. This nation is in a state that it cannot be recovered from: the hatred, the drugs, the decrepit acceptance of gay and transsexuals as normal. All of this will be their demise. I want nothing to do with saving them. Nothing at all!"

"Okay," Mahammed said. "I just don't see the point in not fulfilling your goals."

"I have," DeShawn went on, "they took away so much in my life. Through their books and schooling, I took back what I needed."

"Okay, I guess," Mahammed said, "all that is left is, do you really need to present this?"

"Yes," DeShawn said.

The following Thursday, DeShawn stood, prepared to defend his thesis before the panel. As he did, he could see the shocked faces around the room. When he finished, there was dead silence.

Dean Moore looked at DeShawn and said, "Wow and more wow! DeShawn, why? Why would you present this? Even if this is true, and even if it was relevant, it could not be published or accredited. It's a complete waste of your vast knowledge. You have the greatest mind to ever come through our department. To make a complete mockery of this department and Temple University will not be condoned. DeShawn, I cannot do anything but to withdraw your scholarship immediately. All I can say is, go! You have dishonored Mahammed and Omar! I hope you got what you wanted!"

"By the grace of Allah, I hope you get what you deserve!" DeShawn said. With that, he grabbed his stuff and left.

Mahammed met him outside. "Well?" he asked.

DeShawn said, "Well, it went like I thought. They not only failed my defense but they also kicked me out of the program. They didn't entertain any part of it."

"It must be Allah's plan," Mahammed told DeShawn. "Maybe this escalates our move to Syria sooner than later. I will pray on it."

After prayers on the morning of February 3, 2015, DeShawn went to his room, gathered a large duffle bag he packed the night before and went to the car Mahammed was waiting by, along with Ahmed.

"Have a safe trip. It has been a great joy. You two will be sorely missed. Please stay in touch," Ahmed told them.

And with that, they were off to the airport.

CHAPTER VI

It was early morning on February 30. DeShawn and Mahammed walked on the tarmac at London's Heathrow Airport. Mahammed told DeShawn not to wander off because it was only an hour until they were to board a connecting flight to Warsaw in Poland. He warned DeShawn not to lose touch with his passport.

"Now that you are out of America, your passport needs to be protected at all times. It assures you an easy passage. I will get our tickets confirmed and will meet you at the food court. Get you something to eat."

About fifteen minutes later, DeShawn saw Mahammed heading for him.

"What did you get us?"

"A couple of burgers and some water. Is that okay?" DeShawn asked.

"That's fine. We can eat a real meal when we get to Warsaw. We have a three-hour layover there before we fly into Raqqa. We will stay there a night and then rent a car. The next day, we will head to my home in Tiyas. My family has lived there for three generations."

Finally arriving in Raqqa, DeShawn was amazed at his surroundings. Although he saw several tall buildings, none were nearly as tall as are in America. Mahammed showed him the city gates. He explained they had stood for centuries and had lived through countless conflicts. "Many buildings have come and gone, but now what you see is mostly built by Sunnis. Years earlier, most non-Sunni buildings were destroyed by ISIS. They ravaged this area, destroying most of the historical relics. Prior to the time of the Muslim, they cleansed the land. So now all you see is true to Allah. Enough talk. Now let me treat you to a real dinner."

Mahammed and DeShawn went to a nice place, none like DeShawn had ever seen. The walls were stone laid and sun baked. The roof was made of metal with some white paint but mostly rusted. He noticed the wood-fired ovens inside. They sat outside under an awning at a small table.

"Let's start with some nice Arabic coffee and some Za Latar. It is delicious! It comes with minced meat and cheese manakish." Once the order was placed, Mahammed told DeShawn, "You now must try my favorite since I was a child. Shish kebob. It's not like the one in America. We make them with stuffed zucchini and stuffed yabra. They are grape leaves. Delicious! You will see!!"

The food was good but to truly enjoy, DeShawn would have to let it grow on him a bit. But he told Mahammed it was delicious. What was delightful was the baklava. It came full of chopped nuts, soaked in honey. They ate them while sipping white coffee.

"I'm stuffed! Let's go before I burst!" Mahammed said.

He led DeShawn on a short stroll along the banks of the Euphrates River. DeShawn took it all in. Then they went back to the hotel.

DeShawn was glad it was modern, with the exception of the TV. No English. So he sat and read his book.

The next morning, DeShawn and Mahammed walked to the airport. The car rental was right next door. Mahammed went inside to rent a car. He came back with a Nissan key.

"We have AC! Thank Allah! It will be needed greatly! We will travel mostly desert."

"No American cars?" DeShawn asked.

Mahammed said, "No American anything. That was your past."

The trip through the desert was boring. The same scenery: sand. Mahammed told DeShawn about the great wars. How the Sunnis held off the Kurds, how joining with ISIS held back the Americans and inflicted great destruction on them.

As they approached Tiyas, DeShawn could see planes landing. He asked why they didn't land here.

"It's a military base. The Syrian Air Force uses it. No others are permitted. Stay clear. The less they know of us, the better."

As they approached Mahammed's house, he could see it was boarded by a stone wall. The house was made of stone with a clay tile roof. The yard was sand.

"This is home," Mahammed said. "This is what I came back to re-build. A month ago, the Israelites raided the airport but instead bombed my house. This is a way of life. It is our constant struggle."

The house was nice inside. It had elegant rugs on the floor but it was distinctly missing furniture. All of the beds were made, mattresses lying on the floor.

Functional, DeShawn thought.

It had a modern kitchen with many new appliances. Mahammed told DeShawn he was considered fortunate.

"Many years of war across the country have left so many with so little. We will stay here until my brothers come. They know I'm here but when will they show up, who knows. They travel as nomads so no one can trace them. The way they love, so shall you."

The next few days were uneventful. DeShawn would sit outside reading a book and occasionally watch a fighter jet land or take off. One the third evening, DeShawn was awoken from his sleep by Mahammed.

"They are here. It's time to rise."

"Now?" DeShawn asked.

"You will get used to it. It is the way. Train at night, hide during the day. If they see you during the day, you will have a gun pointed in their direction."

DeShawn walked out of his room to find five men of Arabic decent, all wearing turbans and donning Arabic attire.

"This is the young man I spoke of."

All the men laughed.

"This is the man with the brain and muscles of ten men? He is a boy in western wear! He will die in the first month!"

"Don't be so quick to judge! He has been through much in his young life. He has gained great faith."

"Okay," said the tall Arab fighter. He looked at DeShawn. "My name is Abduol. You will come with me to learn our ways. You will learn to fight as we have. You will be trained the way we have and the way our fathers were trained. Do you accept this? I must warn you that it is not an easy life. You will be conditioned to walk miles in the desert with no water. You will learn to track the enemy and, if necessary, wait for days to kill the infidel. Do you accept?"

DeShawn went blank for a second and then said, "Yes. It will be for Allah."

Abduol responded, "Okay. Please get him out of those clothes! Dress him correctly!"

Within an hour, the six disappeared into the darkness. Abduol led the group away, traveling to the east through the desert. Never stopping. Never talking. DeShawn could make out mountains ahead.

As daybreak approached, they began climbing until DeShawn could make out an opening in the rocks (a cave).

AbDoul finally spoke. "We're home."

DeShawn didn't know what to expect. Inside the cave, about a hundred feet in, the cave opened up to a large room (probably fifty feet in diameter that rose about twelve feet). Around the area, he saw mattresses and sleeping bags. Randomly, around the middle, was a large rug. DeShawn assumed it was for meetings. At the entrance, there was a firepit for cooking.

AbDoul told the men to lay down their gear. "I'll alert you outside for prayers. DeShawn, you stay with me. Daytime, we sleep. Get to know the men. After evening prayers, we start for the first week. You shadow Daniel. He started three months ago. He is from England. He wished to join the cause through his mosque. Life here is hard but we must always train to keep our sacred way of life. Come, let me introduce you to our group."

After prayers, DeShawn sat in the middle of the cave with Daniel and three others while the rest formed various pods. Everyone appeared to be talking about the events of the day. Daniel told DeShawn the group that came to guide him back were part of the leadership. Everyone else were trainees.

"They are strict," Daniel explained, "but they are very good. They will push you to find out what you are capable of. See those three over there? They have shown little skill. They are being trained differently. I think maybe suicide bombing but it's just a guess. They say very little about anything upcoming. Every now and then, a group will visit camp. When that happens, we learn of their great accomplishments. Once a week, a jeep delivers supplies. We will stay here until we are worthy to join the cause. Don't wander off. Last week, one who wished to join tried to leave. AbDoul said it was okay. As the man started to walk into the desert, AbDoul told us to have target practice. So I guess you know how that ended. You must get some sleep. The nights are long. You need all your energy."

The squad awoke to AbDoul summoning them to evening prayers. Afterwards, they sat down and ate falafel and hummus with tea to drink. There was also a plate with cheese and jams. Whoever was the cook, he was good. Afterwards, they were led higher up the mountain until they were on a plateau. There were various obstacles along the walls. The group pulled them out and stared assembling them. They included various climbing apparatuses but mainly targets. Training began by running and exercises, followed by obstacles. DeShawn was issued an AK5-744 assault rifle. It was light but DeShawn had never held a gun since he shot his dad, let along fired one.

"Daniel, show him the operation and how to fire the gun. DeShawn, you will be given one week to not only be shooting but to be able to disassemble and reassemble the gun in under five minutes."

DeShawn shook his head. Daniel told DeShawn it wasn't hard.

DeShawn told him, "That's my kind of task."

Over the next few months, DeShawn really excelled in his training. He grew strong, mastering assault weapons of all sort. He really liked the AK-308. It was a Russian sniper gun. The accuracy was amazing. He loved to calculate the target in wind and distance. All of this was noticed by AbDoul, who conveyed his observations to his superiors.

The following week, AbDoul received an encrypted message on his satellite phone to move DeShawn to Al-Rawdah for training in explosives.

AbDoul messaged back: "Are you sure? He will be a great fighter."

"Yes" the message came back. "We need new minds and fresh ideas if we want to progress."

"It will be done," AbDoul messaged back.

The next evening, they headed out. AbDoul led the way.

"It will take two nights of travel to get there but continue your training. The powers-to-be believe you are capable. Where you go to is a facility only few know about. Al-Rawdah has only a few locals. It is an ancient site. A few settlers remained after the archeologists left. This compound is 90% underground. So all work goes undisturbed. I have been told you have a great wealth of knowledge. We need new blood in our battle with all the infidels. The western world is creeping ever closer to us. We need new blood for better results in our war."

They made camp the following day. They set up tents, which were the color of sand to camouflage them to any air traffic. They rested for the night travel. AbDoul told DeShawn the compound was about six hours further to the west.

"But, as always, we must not be tracked to the compound. It has to remain secret."

DeShawn thought, *Who would see our way? I have not seen a single light in our trek all night.*

"There are eyes everywhere," AbDoul told him.

They finally arrived at the compound, although walking up to it, it couldn't be made out. AbDoul had a handheld GPS locator. That was his way of finding it. The land was barren and lacked markers to find the way. You couldn't even make it out. Walking up to it, once they got closer DeShawn could make out a mound of sand with a window, barely visible, facing east. This had to be so prayers could be held. They entered through a hatch to the left and climbed down a ladder. Once inside, it was amazing. The huge space was well lit. It had air conditioning too. There were lab stations throughout with glass walls looking into other areas. AbDoul led the group through a corridor and entered into a meeting room. It had a large table with many chairs. AbDoul pulled a chair out and asked DeShawn to sit.

Four men entered the room. All wore turbans but they all donned lab coats.

"Glad to see you," AbDoul said to the older of the four men. "DeShawn, I would like you to meet Bakir Faraj. He is the leader of the compound. Habib Ishiaq is to his immediate right. Then you have Jamech Ismail and Jafer Majid. They are the great comrades. I have known all a very long time." AbDoul went on, "Well, this is DeShawn. In front of you is the report that came from Ayatollah El Fazaza."

They all looked briefly at AbDoul and then back at the briefing minutes.

AbDoul told them what they had in front of them was put together by Mahammed Majid. "What you will read is quite incredible. It explains all of this young man's upbringing. It also tells of his incredible aptitude for learning. Mahammed also exploits DeShawn's faith and undying path to serve Allah and our cause. Because of DeShawn's upbringing in America, along with his vast knowledge of their culture he is invaluable to the cause. But what he really brings to us is the understanding of how America ticks, the infrastructure, the inner workings of America. We need him to know what your team knows. Once you feel he has learned our tools to date, you only contact Ayatollah El Fazaza. This is confidential."

"I understand," Bakir said.

AbDoul looked at DeShawn and said, "DeShawn, when we first met and I saw you hold that gun on the first day, I imagined you walking out in the desert in one week. But you have proven to me your abilities. I only wish we could arm an army such as you. Hopefully, we meet again. Praise Allah! Now I must go back."

Bakir looked at DeShawn. "You are so young. We never see a man so young. Usually it is late 20s or 30s they develop. Here you will learn explosives. Different ways to make them, different materials from everyday to sophisticated explosives. We will read the paperwork. Then tomorrow we start. You go with Jafar. He will show you around. See you in the morning."

They all bowed slightly and left the room.

Jafar, the youngest of the group, told DeShawn, "Relax. You will be treated like royalty here. They need our work. We teach everyone how to blow things up. Very fun stuff. No other job lets you blow things up while they treat you as a prince. I am studying the different substances that react with ammonia nitrate. It's quite fascinating! I will show you tomorrow. Now let's teach you the compound. You must be hungry."

DeShawn's quarters were nice. He even had a TV, although there wasn't much to watch, but he would be able to catch up on what was going on in the world. DeShawn walked back to the library and picked out several books. It seemed like months since he was able to read anything but the Koran. He went back to shower and finally settled in for the evening.

The following morning, DeShawn went for prayers. It was odd that they prayed facing the window but he would get used to it. In their dining hall, he was filled with glee to find cereal and milk. *Wow! Amazing!* he thought.

Bakir took DeShawn with him to show him the current work in progress. "We all take different approaches but we all collaborate together. Wednesday, we meet and discuss the week's findings. Jafar studies and tests ammonia nitrate. Habib is on the other side of the lab. You can see he is working on detonators. He is currently exploring more options using cell signals. Jameel, who is in the area you see through the glass, works on biochemicals. That room is a containment cell. You make sure you understand fully all precautions for entering and exiting that area. So to start, why don't you begin by assisting Jafar? You will find it fascinating. My hope is that your knowledge of existing infrastructure will help pinpoint the types of detonations we are shooting for."

DeShawn told Bakir how much fun he thought all of it would be but asked, "Is it possible to get some different reading material? Your books are outdated."

Bakir said, "Definitely! We are under orders to help you find your next level. But you must know, anything you request will take at least a week to obtain. With that done, let's do some work."

Over the next five years, DeShawn dug headlong into the experiments and testing at the compound. Everyone there was amazed at his capacity to learn. But that wasn't the only thing. He also had the ability to push others around him to put the experiments to real practice applications. The results were staggering! A plan was starting to form in his development.

Bakir called DeShawn to his office so the two could discuss his future. Bakir looked at DeShawn and said, "I have had numerous conference calls with the Ayatollah over the last few months. El Fazaza and myself feel little more is to be learned from your training. DeShawn, we feel it is time you met with the Ayatollah to discuss your future, understand your dreams and know your plan. He has dispatched a band of fighters to lead you to his compound. The location is very kept secret. So even once you arrive, the location won't be known, even to you. Is this acceptable?"

DeShawn said, "Yes, this will be my greatest honor! To finally meet the Ayatollah! I have prayed daily to finally serve Allah with all my abilities. I'm highly honored that so many of my brothers find me worthy to meet this great man!"

Bakir told DeShawn, "Then gather your belongings. Tonight, after prayers, you leave."

After prayers, DeShawn met six men, all in black with turbans covering all but their eyes.

"I'm Rafah. I lead this group. You will travel with us to meet El Fazaza. We travel fast and only at night. No sound. No light. We sleep under cover during the day. No sound. The journey will take four days. So if you don't have any questions, get your gear. We leave in fifteen minutes."

DeShawn got his gear and was met by Bakir Habib, Jameel and Jafar at his door. "I will miss you all," DeShawn told them. "Thank you for teaching me all of your wisdom. It will be put to use." With that, he headed off behind RaFah.

The next morning, they arrived at their camping spot. It was a sand dune with a flat side facing the east. The men positioned a tarp (the color of sand) to provide shade and would be like a part of the sand dune to anyone from a distant location. They were only out long enough for morning prayers. Then it was back under cover. The men did not speak. They hurriedly laid out bedrolls and ate what DeShawn thought to be jerky, although he thought it was better not to ask what it actually was. DeShawn couldn't help but to ask Rafah about the squad.

Rafah looked irritated but answered, "This squad has been handpicked by El Fazaza himself. We form his personal staff."

"But what do you do?" DeShawn asked.

Rafah answered, "Whatever is asked, all in the name of Allah. Now, no talking! We travel in silence! No detection whatsoever!"

On the fourth evening, close to dawn, DeShawn could make out a compound in the distance.

Rafar told DeShawn, "We are here. Keep your head covered and stay kneeling until asked to rise in the presence of the Ayatollah."

DeShawn shook his head, saying he understood.

The inside of the compound was massive, with a huge courtyard in the middle. The inside was adorned with ornate tapestries and huge vases that were very elaborate. Rafah showed DeShawn his room and told him the Ayatollah would summon for him but to stay there until then and rest up. DeShawn was performing his morning prayers when a young girl came to his room and announced to DeShawn that the Ayatollah would like his presence. She told him to follow her.

They approached the courtyard, which was set up with a table and four chairs. DeShawn took it to be the Ayatollah that was sitting there with a red-and-white turban and white clothes. DeShawn kept his head bowed.

The Ayatollah raised his hand and told DeShawn to please sit where he gestured. "Let's talk. You are the young man I have heard so much about? How old are you?"

DeShawn answered, "Twenty-four."

"That is so amazing for the knowledge you have grasped in so few years. We have prayed for new blood with insight for a long time. And for someone with the knowledge of western culture is priceless. Please, DeShawn, I must know your vision. How you feel you can help make our great accomplishments better."

DeShawn looked at the Ayatollah and asked, "May I speak my mind, my vision?"

"Yes, please," the Ayatollah answered.

DeShawn paused in awe of his presence. "I have always thought that to bring the West to their knees, a different approach is needed. With all the great accomplishments, little is gained. The West never truly suffers. However little they suffer, they bring one hundred fold the suffering back on the people of Islam. Look at 9/11. We destroyed many lives but it brought the infidels to our land by the thousands. But to most people in America, all it was is sad. It never touched most people. When we bomb or plan many of our operations, the FBI or CIA have intercepted or know enough about the chatter to stop or alter our objective. A different approach is needed. We need to be implanted in America. Not in America as you think. We must implant operatives in rural America, out of sight to lead normal lives, normal American jobs, and gather material in small amounts. In America, cameras are everywhere. The Internet connects and tracks everything. When our plan is to take place, it must disrupt everyone's lives, no deaths. This does no one good. We need to disrupt their everyday life in a way that the people of America destroy America, not the people of Islam."

"How do you propose to do this?" the Ayatollah asked.

"First, I need twenty-five of the most trusted from all your men. We will vow not to use electronics of any type. I will train them. We will, one by one, immigrate to the United States. We will scatter strategically across America and then set up our lives. In five years, once we are accepted and established, we will carry out my plan. Trust me. The shallow lives of western culture is taken easily if you take from them what they have. If you disrupt their power to travel, their ability to communicate, they will turn on the government and then destroy themselves."

"Is this possible?" the Ayatollah asked.

"Yes. Over the next few months, as I train our group, you will see my plan."

The Ayatollah replied, "I will handpick your men from the very men that protect me. They would lay down their lives to do my bidding."

"But hear me," DeShawn said, "no one must see our training and planning. Only you will know our plan and only you will know when we attack, even as it develops."

"Then it shall be," the Ayatollah said, "but I must know your plan in its entirety."

"Fine," DeShawn replied.

"Take today as a day of rest," the Ayatollah said. "Tomorrow you will meet the men I pick. I will think on how to select them and where and how you train them. We will talk often. So please, enjoy your day."

DeShawn awoke the next day for prayers. As he entered the court, he noticed two BM-21 covered trucks. He thought it odd but went to prayers.

After prayers, DeShawn went to the courtyard. He suddenly saw a large group of men. With them was the Ayatollah. Standing beside him, to DeShawn's surprise, were Omar and Mahammed. *Wow!* DeShawn thought.

The Ayatollah told DeShawn, "These men have always been in my inner circle. They have always been fighters for Allah. That's how I'm able to know your story. I know in my heart that because of the suffering you experienced through your young life, you will remain true to the cause."

DeShawn asked, "But why didn't you tell me all of this?"

Mahammed explained, "That would not have let you complete your journey. Your destiny needed you to evolve."

Ayatollah replied, "These are your men. All speak fluent English."

"But my plans require twenty-five men who are able to travel to America on visas. Who are the rest?" DeShawn asked.

"We have given you fifty to teach and train: twenty-five for your needs and twenty-five more if your plan is successful to carry on for Allah." Omar told DeShawn, "Each new idea, they must double the effort. The people of Islam must stop fighting each other and band together. This will be how to get the western cultures from randomly calling wars and coming to our nations and slaughtering our fighters and our families."

"Do you agree to this?" the Ayatollah asked. "Your plan will go as you explained it to us. It is a plan so simple but so complex that the men you train must execute it precisely. It will be hard for the westerners to know and understand what hit them. These men will travel east with you to a compound near Marqada. There you will have your six months to teach the men what you know. The covered trucks you see are equipped with rocket launchers. The men are the best soldiers we have. They have sworn an oath that they will lay their lives down for Allah and your quest. I hope that is not needed. My plan, my goal, is for Arabs to stop. My hope is for Arabs to serve Allah in peace and tranquility. Let the westerners suffer great! May we bring them to their knees!"

"Good luck, son!" the three exclaimed. "We will be here to greet you six months from now. Then the plan starts."

Over the new six months, DeShawn taught the group his whole plan. He explained everything: how they were to live in America, how DeShawn would give them their orders. He greatly expressed the need for absolutely no communication on the Internet. He explained how they would live and gather the needed materials to carry out his plan. He taught them that all they would need could be gathered slowly, as not to be detected.

"Every day, you must be aware. In America, every word, every stop you take is being watched. You must be nice and sociable to everyone you meet for my plan to be executed. You must fit in and be totally accepted to all around you. Any suspicion and the plan will fail. This will not be easy." He added, "This plan will take five years to work but in the end, we will bring hell on earth to the infidels who look at us as savages."

His time passed quickly. Finally, at the age of 25 in the fall of 2021, the convoy of men arrived back at the compound to reunite with the Ayatollah.

Inside the compound, the Ayatollah greeted them. "I am sorry, DeShawn. Omar and Mahammed were summoned back to America. They expressed their sorrow that they would miss your return. Now come! Let's go discuss the last six months and the future to come!"

DeShawn told the Ayatollah, "The plan needs to start now. Here is a list of locations you must send a man to in order to set up bank accounts. Each account must have $50,000 available to each man. Here is a list of names that go with each account. The man must travel by car and pay for his travel completely with cash. No trail can link each location to the other. The men will scatter out across Europe and take random flights to the United States. All are taught to be openly friendly. Each have been given instructions on how to dress and the western mannerisms so that they will blend in fast. This is a list of men I picked for my mission. All the men took the training. I feel all grasped what I was teaching. The next five years will be crucial to our success. May Allah be praised! I leave in two weeks. Your only correspondence will be to this name at a postal box. I will tell Omar its place. All conversations for the next five years will be this way. I hope that one day I'll be able to see you again."

"I hope the same to you, DeShawn," the Ayatollah exclaimed. "I will pray every day for your success. Go with Allah. Make us proud!"

CHAPTER VII

AUGUST 12, 2021

DeShawn arrived at the Hartsfield-Jackson International Airport. He cleared customs easily. The TSA agent looked up at DeShawn after seeing the country DeShawn passed through but let him pass. Nonetheless, DeShawn called for an Uber to take him to Roswell, a medium-sized town north of Atlanta.

I must get my driver's license, he thought as he awaited the car to arrive. *That will be my first task besides a place to live.*

He booked a room at the Marriott Extended Stay. It was nice and had all he needed while finding a place.

The next day, he traveled to the DMV downtown. Along the way, he noticed a bicycle shop. He would stop there on the way back. Inside the DMV, they told him he was in luck. If he passed the written exam today, they had an opening for a driving test tomorrow.

"How great!" DeShawn told the lady behind the counter. "Let's do this!"

Of course, the written exam was passed. So he told the lady he would be back tomorrow. She told him to be there by 9:30 and the examiner would take him driving at 10:00. DeShawn shook his head that he understood and decided to go back and visit the bike shop.

On the way, he saw an ice cream parlor across the street. He had to go there! He couldn't remember the last time he had tasted ice cream.

"A double scoop of strawberry," he told the young girl working behind the counter. He was thinking, *How great!*

As he exited the store, he bumped straight into a man who was with his wife and got strawberry ice cream on his shirt. The man's eyes shot fire at him!

"Just great!" the man exclaimed. "You would think your type might one day pay attention! But no!!! Your type doesn't learn!"

DeShawn apologized but the man would hear nothing of it as his wife dabbed at the ice cream.

"Just leave!" the man exclaimed. "Go crawl back to where you came from! Worthless! Just worthless!"

DeShawn said he was sorry again and backed out of the situation. Now he no longer wanted to visit the bike shop. He just wanted to go back to his room and look for a job. The people of America had not changed. Not at all!

Back at his room, he turned on the TV to get caught up in the world. It was as if he never left! The murder rate was escalating, hate crimes, mass killings, rioting in Washington, etc. He turned the news off. The infidels never change. The hatred never leaves. But it would!

"I will stop when I take all they have away. I'll just wait!"

He started researching top engineering companies in Atlanta and settled on submitting his resume to three firms, all mechanical engineering firms. During his trip to the States, he had put his resume together since he had a lot of extra time to waste. But after submitting the resume on his iPad, there was little to do but hope for a call.

The next day, DeShawn walked out of the DMV with license in hand. He walked through the town to scope out what was there. He did find what he was hoping for, a Walmart. He walked into the store and went to the electronics department. He purchased a cheap phone and the cheapest calling plan possible and then left. Outside, he dialed the number Omar had given him. He left a short message: "Meet me in three days, Saturday, August 17, at 2:00 P.M. at the City Barbeque on the corner of Main and 3rd streets in Roswell, GA." Then he hung up.

DeShawn walked into the alley, threw the phone on the ground, smashed it with his foot, scooped it up and threw its pieces into two separate dumpsters. He then turned and went straight to a Buy Here, Pay Here Auto Dealership. He looked around the lot at the cars and saw what he was looking for. It was a worn 2012 Subaru. It had a few dents but looked okay. The salesman told him it was a one-owner vehicle but DeShawn knew better. He just wanted something to drive that no one would look at.

They sat down and DeShawn told the salesman he had no credit but he had half the price of the car to put down. The salesman asked why he had no job history. DeShawn told him that after he graduated college, he traveled Europe. The salesman filled out the paperwork and told DeShawn that if he missed one payment that he could kiss the money goodbye. DeShawn shook his head that he understood. He grabbed the paperwork and the keys and left.

He decided to drive around the outskirts of town in search of a rental. His plan was working. Two days later, DeShawn received an email from McNeil Enterprises (a company specializing in telecommunications) asking DeShawn to come in for an interview on Monday, the 19ᵗʰ, at their corporate office in Atlanta. DeShawn was excited! He left out where he was raised and gave no location of where he received his high school diploma. He left out his time spent at Temple University and relied only on transcripts from Wright State. But he guessed that was enough, at least for an interview.

DeShawn sat quietly in the City Barbeque awaiting Omar. Then he appeared and came over and sat across the table.

"It's been a long time," Omar said. "I hope all finds you well. Is the food good here? Never ate here."

DeShawn said, "Too much to do."

"How can I help?" Omar asked.

"Here is a list of names and documents to set up bank accounts. They are listed by number, as the order of where each will settle and arrive in the country. You only have one month to reach the final city."

Omar glanced at the list. "This is all over the country, every corner!" he exclaimed.

"Yes, and you must drive. Leave no trail. Pay everything in cash. There must be no way to trace the sites to each other. Leave your cell phone at home. Buy burner phones in case you need assistance."

"This is a lot," Omar said.

"I only trust you," DeShawn told him. "We will meet here every year at this time and date. You will bring news from Ayatollah. I will send him our progress. If you do not come every year or if I don't show up, the plan has failed."

"Okay," Omar told him.

"Well, by the grace of Allah, all goes as planned. Until next year, I guess. Good luck."

Then they went their separate ways.

DeShawn arrived at McNeil Enterprises precisely at 1:00 P.M. He told the receptionist that he had an interview with Mr. Klaus. She picked up the phone and told DeShawn to go to the 5th floor, Suite 503. He would be interviewed there.

When DeShawn arrived at the office, the secretary look up and asked, "DeShawn?"

He replied, "Yes, ma'am."

"Mr. Klaus is waiting for you right in there."

DeShawn entered the office and saw a little man with glasses rise from his desk, offering a handshake.

"Please sit," he said.

DeShawn thanked him.

"DeShawn, I read your college transcript. Quite impressive, I must say. But no work history? Can you fill me in on why?"

"Well, sir," DeShawn replied, looking him in the eye, "I felt a need to travel and see the world. I felt that if I didn't fulfill that urge before I started working, I may never get the time."

"Well," Mr. Klaus said, "I like what I'm reading. But I feel, as for entry-level, all I can offer is a paid internship. We can revisit your position in three months, after I know you're capable and adjust accordingly. The position would start out at $80,000 per year, which is quite good for a young man. Would you like to think it over?"

DeShawn said, "No. I will prove my worth to you. I think you have made a generous offer."

"Well, son, report to the Research Department on the 2nd floor, room 221. Ask for Mr. Kline. He will get you started. And if you would, take a few minutes with my secretary to get the paperwork started."

DeShawn rose up and said, "Thank you. You won't be sorry."

After leaving, DeShawn decided to pick back up on his search for a secluded rental. He left feeling his plan was really happening. Riding around the country roads, he stopped at a little gas station at the edge of town. He fueled up and went in to pay. Inside, the store was stacked floor to ceiling with what appeared to be every item, from hardware to food. He looked around a bit and then went to pay for his gas.

He asked the elderly lady, "Any places around this area up for rent?"

She looked up and surprisingly said, "Yep. Probably."

DeShawn eagerly asked her how to find them.

"You need to talk to my husband, Paul. He's home right now."

"Can you give me directions?" DeShawn asked.

"Just call him. His number is right here."

"I don't carry a phone, ma'am," DeShawn replied.

"What's the matter with you, boy? Everyone has a phone!"

"Well, I don't" was his response.

"Okay," the lady answered. She told DeShawn where to drive and how to get there. "When you meet Paul, mind your manners. He doesn't take to your type much but he has been working on it."

"What type?" DeShawn asked.

The lady just pointed to his skin.

"Oh," he replied. "I'll be okay, ma'am."

The place she sent him to was only five minutes away. As he pulled down the drive, DeShawn could make out a large older man bent under the hood of a pickup truck. He turned around, looking visibly bothered by the company.

"Good afternoon, sir," DeShawn said. "The lady at the gas station said you may hold some rental property."

"Nothing you would like," Paul answered.

"You may be surprised," DeShawn replied.

"You have cash? I don't deal with plastic."

"Yes, sir, I do."

"Okay. Hop in the truck. I don't have time to be mess'n around. When you wanting to move in?" Paul asked.

"Right now, if the place suits me. Probably tomorrow."

Paul told him, "Ain't much out here. No cable and the Internet is sketchy at best. Here we are."

They pulled into a long driveway. As they went around a curve, DeShawn saw an old farmhouse. It was in bad need of a paint job. It had a large yard and two out buildings.

"See what I told you? Not up your alley."

DeShawn replied, "No, it's exactly what I was looking for. Can I see inside?"

"I suppose, but I don't have all day."

DeShawn went inside the two-story house. It had some furniture but he could see work needed done. But the place was exactly what his plan called for. Privacy.

"I'll take it," DeShawn told him. "How much?"

"It's $1,400 a month, $1,400 deposit. You miss one day, don't wait for an eviction notice. I'll get you out."

"Okay," DeShawn said.

With that, Paul drove them back. "You can pay your rent at the gas station. The woman you met there is my wife. She will get it to me. About once a month, I'll drive up to see if you are trashing the place. And believe me! Don't let that happen!"

"It won't, sir."

Paul asked, "Why does a young man like yourself want to live out here? I thought you guys like the conveniences of city life."

DeShawn merely replied, "I'm not one of those people. Thank you for your time, sir. I'll bring the money to the gas station tomorrow. Will there be a contract?"

"None of that need with me," Paul responded. "You just do what I say and I'll do what I promised."

As DeShawn was driving away, he thought of how perfect that went, cash transactions and no paperwork, no paper trail. Perfect!

The next day, DeShawn paid the rent as promised and was handed the keys. He drove out to the house to take what little he had and to make a list of what was needed. It was a lot but he did have a few days to settle in before starting work. In the following days, he made huge headway with getting the electric and gas in his name, buying groceries and a few furniture items for the house, especially a bed. He was not sleeping on the bed that was in the house! The place was perfect! No one to watch him performing prayers. No one to watch him assemble items for his plan. He just needed to stay off the radar for the next five years.

His first day at work was unusual. Mr. Kline showed DeShawn the various research labs and the different things they were working on. He asked DeShawn what he was particularly interested in.

DeShawn responded, "Practical applications. I've done research but I really like getting in and seeing things work."

Mr. Kline replied, "You'll start here. If all goes well, we can see about fieldwork. Why don't you help Bill? He is researching methods of boosting cell signals."

"Okay," DeShawn said. "Let's get started."

DeShawn blended well with the group. Over the following months, he fit in well. All was good. Everyone thought he was a good hand.

Back at the farmhouse, one month came up. When he went to pay the rent, the lady looked surprised.

"What?" DeShawn asked. "Did I do something wrong?"

"No," she answered. "Everyone swore you would have been out of there after two weeks!"

"Nope! I'm staying!" DeShawn answered. "Suits me just fine!"

After he left, she couldn't wait to call Paul. He was amazed. Then he told her that maybe he'd just drive out there to take a peek.

When he drove up to the house, he couldn't believe it! The house had about half of the front already repainted. All of the grass was cut and all of the weeds around the out buildings were cut down. He could see DeShawn was at work and decided to leave it alone. After all, the place never looked so good! He thought, *This boy might work out! He even pays rent on time! He must have been raised by white folks.*

Through the months, DeShawn kept being a creature of habit: work, home, occasionally at the feed store, grocery store and, of course, the hardware store. In the first year, he had received two raises and he upgraded his ratty car to a new Toyota pickup truck (gray in color). He secretly made bombs in the outbuildings. His first task was to make a hidden room in the biggest of the two outbuildings. He also had dug a hidden room under the floor to store his items as he made them. He lined the walls with plastic and Styrofoam. This kept everything dry and especially cool. As he was developing the items, his work on the house and ground continued. Now Paul had seen enough of the transformation of the house and grounds. He would nod to De-Shawn when he saw him in passing.

Finally, August 19th came. It was a Friday this year. So DeShawn asked for the day off. He really needed to meet with Omar.

When 2:00 came, like clockwork Omar strolled into the City Barbeque.

"Let's have lunch but after, we will go to my place so we can speak in privacy."

"Okay," Omar said.

Omar was impressed at the secluded house DeShawn had. "This is nice," he said.

"It didn't when I got here. I'm keeping the redneck owner from coming around. He's getting something for nothing. So he isn't going to ask questions."

"Smart," Omar replied.

"Now to business," DeShawn continued. "Did you bring the addresses?"

"Right here," responded Omar. "You really made it difficult to get the bank accounts set up, but we made it happen by just one day before we had to. Also, here is a letter from each, explaining how they're doing, all unopened, just as you wanted. I only received one phone call asking for additional money. He had trouble finding a job in Butte Montana but it was only once. So I think all is good now."

"Here is the letter I need sent to the Ayatollah. Don't mail it until you're closer to Philadelphia. Mail it from a truck stop. You understand? That's all I can tell you. I will not need you anymore. We are established. All you do now is wait until the day. It's May 11, 2027. It is going to be a day to celebrate! A day all our people will remember! Omar, you have been a great friend! Go in peace."

With that, Omar got in his car and drove off.

The next few years were uneventful, on purpose. DeShawn enjoyed getting letters from all the men and seeing how they were progressing. All seemed to be following true to the discussed plan. All were well blended into the communities and not doing anything to raise suspicion. From what DeShawn could understand by some of the cryptic phrases was that most, if not all, of the needed materials they would use were already gathered. Each of them had stored away much of the money they would need for the final stage. From what DeShawn also gathered from the letters was the explosives were easy for everyone to get and to assemble. The detonators were more problematic. Many ended up buying other electronics to get the parts needed. Burner phones were purchased as timers but none of the phones would be activated until the final stage of the plan was reached.

One day in October 2020, while on his visit to the post office, he tipped his hat to the postal worker behind the counter weighing mail.

When the man looked up, he said hi to DeShawn and asked, "Can I ask you something? Everyone else around here may get a couple of handwritten letters a year. But you get them constantly from all over the States and all the time. That's bazaar."

DeShawn calmly told him that it was a pact he had made with his fraternity brothers from college.

"That's really unique," the man said. "You guys really kept it up! Good for you! Sorry to bother you. Have a nice day," he concluded.

"Good day to you too," DeShawn added. Then he left.

That was the only questioning he received from the locals. Not bad considering the five years he spent in a town of mostly white people.

DeShawn spent the next two months compiling a list of targets that he would send to each man. With each target, he would give a precise time and date for it to detonate, along with the type of charge. On January 15, 2027, the letters were complete, along with one special letter he would mail later to the Ayatollah. In each letter were instructions in specific regards to targets but each were individual. So if one member drew attention, no information would be known of any other pulling off the plan. Each were told to put in a notice saying they were resigning by the second week of March. They were to keep their places of residence to return. Each of their targets were picked to be within a day's drive. They were told how and when they would be traveling. The day was March 29th. From this time on, DeShawn wouldn't know results until the morning of May 11th. So after all the letters went out, nothing would be left to do but to wait and hope that all of the time and planning would bring this nation to their knees.

CHAPTER VIII

It was early Tuesday. The nation went on as usual. People arriving to work, scurrying around. At the Washington Office of Homeland Security, it was now 8:45 A.M. A group of secretaries and officers all stood in front of the bulletin board joking.

"Cover your head!"

"Run for the hills!"

"I'm calling my wife!"

Dan walked toward them and said, "Alright! That's enough! Back to work! We have a country to protect."

Everyone hustled back to their stations. At 9:05 A.M., the phone lines erupted. As everyone hustled to answer them, the look on everyone's faces was shocking! Dan came out of his office to see what was disrupting the office.

Mark Collins' desk was the closet to Dan's office. He heard him asking, "What? How bad? No way! This can't be happening! Okay, let me get going on this fast!" Mark turned to Dan and said, "You are not going to believe this! This is fucking insane!" He went on to tell Dan that at exactly 9:00 A.M., a series of explosions took place at the Marathon Ashland Refinery in Detroit, MI. The place was exploding everywhere and fireballs could be seen for miles. It was a complete catastrophe!

Dan surveyed his office. Two cubicles to the left of Mark, Dan noticed Paula hang up the phone and put her hands on her cheeks. Dan asked Paula what she heard. Paula told him that a series of up to five explosions happened in rural Idaho, maybe a mile apart, sending huge fireballs into the sky.

Dan's brain was reeling. Then he raised his voice and addressed the staff, "People, each of you finish your phone calls. Gather as much information as possible. Then meet me in the Situation Room! ASAP!"

One by one, the room filled in ten minutes.

Dan asked for a big map of the United States and started inserting pins at various locations. In addition to pins being placed in Detroit, MI, he stuck one south of Weber, UT, and then one west of Elko, NV. Then he sat in a chair and said, "It's time to call the president. Mark, you continue on. This has to be complete within the hour."

Dan went to his office and called the president. The phone picked up and he heard, "Yes, Dan. What can I help you with?"

Dan told him, "Sir, I have very grave news. We are compiling information. It's very early to understand. All I can give you is a vague description. But it appears we are under a very strange attack. The locations are dotted all over the nation. It will take a while to figure out the exact locations and even longer to realize the impact. The only real piece of information is that it is about refined oil and the distribution. I will have a more detailed account of the situation within the hour. In the meantime, let's let the reports float in."

The president replied, "Get what you can. I will assemble the Security Council."

Dan returned to the Situation Room and immediately started to panic. He looked at the map and asked, "How many? Is this all?"

Mark looked at Dan and said he hoped.

"Well, let's put something together the best we can. I have one hour to address the Security Council. I want all top investigators in here now!" Dan paused for a moment to peer at the map and then started asking questions. "In addition to the refinery in Detroit, MI, are there others that are affected?"

Mark stepped up to the map. "Yes," he replied. "There appears to be four, all lit at exactly 9 A.M., all by explosives. Definitely by someone who knew how to effectively shut operations down and possibly for a while, depending on how quick we can put out fires and contain secondary explosions."

"What about the other pins?" Dan asked. "I see North Carolina, Arizona, Colorado, Idaho and Pennsylvania. What do these represent?"

Mark responded, "Dan, these are equally disturbing. The locations are all remote and each is a major gasoline pipeline. Each location had a series of five explosions, approximately a quarter-mile apart. And Dan, all explosions happened at 9:00 A.M. precisely."

Dan just looked at Mark and the rest of the investigators. Then he walked directly to the bulletin board to rip down the email everyone had so much fun with.

Dan returned to the Situation Room, walked over to the map and pinned the message right over Washington. Then he turned and said, "Could this possibly be our lead? How could this be carried out without a whiff of Intel? No chatter? How is this scale of attack in such a wide area? This makes no sense! I have to meet with the

Security Council. Let's get all the facts in now! I leave for a meeting at the White House in two hours!!!"

DeShawn sat intently in front of his TV at 9 A.M. on the morning of May 11th, staring to see how or if it would be reported. Then, at 9:25 A.M., a Special Report came across the screen. All it said was: "Reports are coming in from across the country that a series of explosions occurred simultaneously at 9:00 A.M. It appears all were connected but no other information was available at this time."

DeShawn sat there, pleased with himself and ecstatic at how the plan played out. He sat there and started writing a letter to all the comrades. Each letter merely stated: "Phase One, complete! Move straight to Phase Two! Be strong and praise Allah!"

He carefully sealed all the letters securely and then went to his truck to mail them from Atlanta.

MAY 11, 2027

At 2:00 P.M., Dan McCarthy strolled into the office that held the Security Council. Seated at the large table were Jim Borlan, the President of the United States; Howard McFarland, Head of the CIA; Josh Jordan, Head of the FBI; and Carl Reed, Chief of Staff. They sat at the head of a table that was filled with numerous members of the different branches of the military. Dan quietly sat down.

Jim Borlan suddenly spoke up, "Well, out with it! What the hell is going on, Dan?"

Dan stood up and started, "At this point, we know very little. We won't know when we can fully assess the situation. My agents are compiling information as we speak. I should be able to give a complete summary by 9:00 P.M. tonight or at least be able to tell what we know at that point."

Jim asked, "What do you know at this point?"

Dan went on. "It appears to be a timed attack that was precisely set off. It seems pointed to destroy the distribution of gasoline. Several refineries have had massive destruction. It's early but we feel some of the remote locations are of large gasoline pipelines. We will have a better idea of the scope at 9:00 P.M. tonight."

"Do you have any idea of who is responsible? What chatter have we heard?" Jim asked.

Dan began, "Mr. President. At this time—and please, this is early—this is a major interruption to the gasoline supply. This could potentially halt shipment of gasoline to 70% of the country. At this time, there is no idea of what timeline for repair will be. But, if it's anywhere close to what we think, this will be the most major impact to the population of the United States we have ever witnessed! Potentially larger than 9/11. But sir, you have to understand that it is early. The blasts could have merely caused minor damage. We just don't know yet."

Dan broke in. "Have you picked up any chatter? Have any clues?"

"The only thing we have at this point is a letter that somehow was received at my office on May 9th. It was so disturbing that it was dismissed as ridiculous. I have a copy of the letter being handed to each of you to read now. Sir. Understand as you read this that, at the time, we felt this handwritten letter had nothing to back it up out there. That it was just totally ridiculous. But now, if this turns out to be the source, one must only ponder what happens in thirty days."

Jim rose and said, "Gentlemen, I want everyone sitting at this table to put the full power of every resource this country offers to figure out this problem and get it corrected. And do it NOW! This meeting is dismissed until 9:00 P.M. tonight! Gentlemen, please exhaust all possibilities!"

And with that, they left.

Dan went back to the Situation Room at Homeland Security to see what developments had come in. As he entered the Situation Room, it appeared to be completely chaotic!

"Report!" Dan demanded.

John spoke up and reported, "Sir, four of our major refinery distributions' piping have been destroyed! This set off explosions that traveled through the refineries. The fires are still being extinguished. The extent of damage won't be known until we are able to get a look. We have also located twenty-two major pipelines in remote locations that we are seeing from the air. They all appear to be ruptured in multiple locations. We have people heading to all locations. We have been able to get to three locations but even with foam, the blazes are still out of control. We stopped the flow of gas. But sir, these are huge two-feet-in-diameter pipelines. It will be a minute until we can get close enough to survey the damage."

"Do we know what this will do for distribution? And how much of the country will be affected? Mark, I want you to take point on that letter. Find out where it came from, who sent it and, most of all, find out how this happened precisely at all these locations without us having a clue! The proximity of the explosions is immense! This could not be just one man! How would such an operation go completely unnoticed? Cindy, I want you to do a map showing each location across the country. I have to give a report at 9:00 P.M. I want everything each of you have by 6:30 P.M. tonight! Everyone get to work!!!"

Each and every one worked frantically to compile as much information as possible. John sent a hundred field agents to the various locations across the county. All offices were given specific instructions as to what their duties were. Mark began to track the letter to see if the handwriting was in any of the databases that collect handwriting descriptions. He also started with the postal stamp and checking for fingerprints. Cindy was busy trying to pinpoint each and every location where the blasts occurred at 9:00 A.M.

At 6:30 P.M., they gathered in the Situation Room. All appeared solemn.

Dan started. "Cindy, let's see the map. Is it complete?"

She replied, "Yes, sir, I believe all locations are on the map. Sir, it's quite unbelievable! Every sector of the country is impacted! Look at the map. The scope of the attacks is unbelievable!"

Dan peered at the map and asked, "How can this happen without anyone knowing? You can't make a phone call, send a message or walk down the street without being seen. Someone has to have Intel on something! Mark! What have you picked up on the letter?"

Mark responded, "Sir, absolutely nothing! We got nothing on the handwriting description. Too many people handled the letter to get anything. All we have is it was mailed from Atlanta, GA, from a mail drop box."

Dan broke in, "I want you to look at any and all cameras surrounding the location of the drop box. I want every image analyzed for any suspicious perps dropping mail. It can't be hard! These days, who would take time to write a letter, let alone send one? John, you're up. What did you get?"

"Well, sir," he replied, "the refineries are about under control. They all seemed to be hit on the distribution pipelines, directly outside the refineries. Then the explosions traveled inside to the production facility. Damage is catastrophic but, given time, rebuildable. The other location was main distribution pipelines that crisscross the country. Each was hit with explosives at various locations. Each location was hit with five bombs placed about one quarter-mile apart. With every location, the place of the blasts were where no cameras are anywhere around. Completely concealed."

"How would they know these locations?"

Dan broke in, "Well, sir, we live in an age of communication, as you see from what is on the board. The Internet has maps of all the pipelines in the world. All of it is public information for the taking."

"Unbelievable! So what's this do to our supply?" Dan asked.

John responded, "Sir, within three days, our gasoline supply will be crippled. Once information is out to the public, I feel a mass rebellion is eminent. People will riot and loot and hoard gas. Panic and chaos. The worst thing is there is no hiding it. No way to control the public."

"Great!" Dan exclaimed. "Well, this should be a meeting of a lifetime tonight when I speak to the president and Security Counsel! Thank you, everyone. Let's get back to work! We have a lot to solve and no time to get it done!"

DeShawn worked quietly in his workshop while listening to the radio. Suddenly, the DJ announced that the president would speak to the public at 10:30 P.M. *Just as planned,* he thought, as he went back to work on finishing another detonator. He had at least a dozen already completed but felt compelled to keep building them. His training had made his task easy. All he had to do was to buy a cheap disposable cell phone and take it apart to alter it so that it could send a charge out at the designated time. The charge was large enough to set off the bombs made from ammonium nitrate and diesel fuel, all easily found materials and materials (if bought in small quantities) would go undetected.

Finishing with detectors, he moved a wooden work desk to the side and uncovered a trap door that hid the cellar where his bombs were stored. Placing the detonator, he looked at his supplies. *Quite the store,* he thought. Looking at his store, he had bombs stored accordingly to what type of explosion he wished to deliver. Some were shaped out of material to explode downwards. Some were shaped merely to blow stuff up. All the men were trained to build similar bombs. All the men knew what to pack and where to go for the next mission. Soon, it would be time to pack his truck for the next mission.

Dan arrived at the Security Council Briefing Room. He set out to hand out folders with the findings and assessment of the day's events. Similar folders had already been placed on the table by the FBI, CIA and armed forces. Everyone was given one half-hour to review the information.

When the president entered the room, everyone rose and waited for orders. The president began, "Gentlemen. I appreciate your efforts. For myself, the members of Congress and the Senate, we lay our trust in you completely. In an hour, I will address the American public with select members of the Congress and Senate. The American public will not take to their lives being disrupted lightly! They will want answers! I'm sorry to say but, as of now, there are no answers to be shared. I saw the vast enormity and extremely complex planning someone or some agency put into this. None seem intent on claiming responsibility. So your task seems enormous with hardly any clues of the culprits being available. In the next few weeks, I expect every agency to continue searching for answers while assisting local and state officials as we are sure of seeing quite the uprising from the American people. News agencies everywhere are speculating on the events and are asking for answers. Please be careful on any information your respected agencies release. Please! I implore you! Let's, for once, work together as one. I think by the nature of the attack, I feel the Department of Homeland Security should take point but in no way do I expect less of any other organization. Do I have your cooperation?"

Everyone in the room hardily agreed to cooperate.

Later at the set press conference, the president laid out the morning's events, step by step. He detailed the scope of the damage. Then he went on to explain the consequences of the attack. He asked the public to remain calm. That the Federal Government would put every asset to repair the damage in the next few days. He went on to tell them it would be a short disruption and to have faith that the full power of the American Government would quickly resolve everything. At that point, he quickly exited the press conference, leaving the select members of Congress and Senate to answer questions. As he was leaving, he told Dan that a daily update of findings must be compiled from each agency and on the Presidential Desk each morning by 9:00 until the country was returned to normalcy. Dan shook his head that he understood and then left to return to his office. There wasn't going to be much sleep tonight, for that matter, many nights.

The next morning, it was mostly quiet across America, although it was noticed that many people had begun to hoard gas by afternoon. Lines were forming at gas stations. People filled their tanks. On top of that, they had additional cans to fill. By late afternoon, there were spotty reports of stations shutting down due to the vast demand. Dan listened to the reports while getting information from the field agents completing their assignment of damage and repair. The reports were all similar. The pipelines were damaged in such a way and in locations where repair would be extremely difficult. All of them had at least two ruptures requiring at a minimum two miles of new pipeline to be installed. Each location would require several weeks, if that, to repair. The refineries, on the other hand, were much worse. The repairs to get them up and running in any capacity would be a month. Also, getting the vast manpower to and from work each day would be problematic with the gas shortage coming. The government was in a much better shape to deal with this since many agencies had been converting many of their fleets to all electric vehicles. The general population was much slower in the conversion. With the cost of the vehicles, it would take years for the public to wean off of gasoline vehicles.

The report read: "Dire Circumstances Ahead." Dan told the president that even though it was a mere two days into the crisis, the president must institute gas rationing. This was surely going to bring a revolt to the general public. The president agreed. Again, the president spoke to the public. After the address, the grumbling of the public could be felt. The people were already demanding answers. But with little than bad news to offer, it seemed silence was the only option. News of the great American tragedy traveled around the world. Many offered assistance. While in the Arab world, they found great satisfaction. Many of the clerics were already preaching that the great country had brought this on themselves and that whoever was behind this must have Allah himself on their side.

As the days progressed with no resolve to get one thing up and running, the public began to protest, calling for action. Some were even calling for a new government. Dan compiled evidence day and night but nothing helped. No one was able to uncover one thing on who or what agency was responsible. On top of that, they were still at least a week from getting the first pipeline repaired.

On the streets, protests were growing bigger and louder. Reports of tanker trucks being stopped and held while gas was being stolen, owners of electric cars reporting vehicles stolen, businesses were closing their doors in huge numbers due to workers being unable to come to work. Lines formed for public transportation and fights broke out due to the availability of passengers. In rural areas where no public transportation was available, many that could use bicycles or horses or else were trapped. In only a week and half, America was falling into disarray.

On the evening of May 20th, the president spoke to the public once again. This time he had good news to spread. During his address he reported, "Through working twenty-four hours a day on every pipeline, and through mobilization of an army of pipefitters, welders and equipment operators, seven of the twenty-two ruptured pipelines will be repaired by the morning (May 22nd). Five more will be up and running three days later. By May 30th, all will be repaired. This will start to heal the country but rationing will remain in effect for at least a month. While repairs to the refineries are being completed, knowing this will not immediately relieve public tension. I beg anyone with any information to come forward. There are no answers coming. The FBI completed their initial investigation into the act and labeled them 'Terrorist in Nature.' Although we have no idea of what organization was involved, they concluded that the attacks were carried out by numerous individuals, located and probably planted for years, across the nation. The bombers all had sophisticated training in explosives, as well as a vast knowledge of our infrastructure. They had knowledge of America's inner workings, how to locate targets, how to avoid cameras and all other tracking gear. They used our own infrastructure to locate specific targets and pinpoint their attacks. It was as simple as a call to 811. They located each and every target. But as to who and why were the attacks were carried out by? No new information on the letter or who was responsible was available. Although the information was useful, it did little to help the current situation.

With the first few pipelines repaired, the unrest of the public did not cease. Riots and looting were being reported in every state of the union. The help of nations sending hundreds of tankers of gasoline to the nation did little. Truckers were not able to get fuel to every corner of the country in a timely manner. This was not going to be a quick fix.

MAY 22, 2027

Meanwhile, back in Roswell, GA, DeShawn began packing gear into his pickup truck. He had no problem with gas. He stockpiled up before the first fuse was ignited. He remained in solitude until the 25th to set up the next lesson for the United States.

On the morning of the 23rd, Dan went to deliver his 9:00 A.M. briefing to the president. Within this briefing, Dan reviewed the only bit of evidence they had. It was the letter from who they believed was responsible for the attacks. He pointed out to the president the fast-approaching date and also what the letter's author had requested from the American public. The president reflected on the briefing and pondered what could possibly be done to appease the author of the letter. With all the discord across the population, how would anything likely to be instituted? If anything, any moves to correct the culture of America would bring more upheaval. Thus, he decided, surely this was a one-time event. No one had that resource for planning or would be able to carry out multiple attacks again. He decided to bring the Chiefs in again and figure the best plan of defense.

The morning of June 4th, everyone was summoned to meet at the Security Council. All had been advised to come up with individual strategies. Dan's team worked through the night before, reading the letter and trying to figure what would be the attacker's next step. Although much was discussed, little was decided. The only solid suggestion was that the 811 call centers around the country would be monitored. Every effort to monitor social media of every type was to be monitored. Then used satellites to watch secluded areas for any activity.

The president stepped in to meet with the Security Council. He began by stating that this had been the hardest month of his life. And, for the first time in his memory, he had no possible solution. Dan proceeded to read their assessment, as each organization did. After, a lengthy discussion was held. Most agreed on the only action possible. Monitor 811, monitor remote areas that had infrastructure relevant to the nation and monitor the Internet.

The president concluded by saying, "I hope this was a one-time event. Let's pray it's true."

JUNE 11TH, 8:55 A.M.

Dan assembled his team to meet in the Situation Room. He told them he thought it best that they be together for 9:00 A.M. Everyone agreed. At 8:58 A.M., Dan requested everyone join him in prayer. When 9:00 came, nothing. At 9:02, lights begin to dim and then went off. The backup generator kicked in. Then the phones went crazy.

CHAPTER IX

Everyone was scrambling to their phones. Dan looked around the room, waiting for a report.

"Cindy!" Dan called out. "Give me what little you know!"

She responded, "Sir, it appears people heard multiple explosions right before their power blacked out. Calls are coming from everywhere. No place was spared."

"Let's get our people moving to figure out how bad it's going to be. It looks like our boy is way ahead of us again."

Cindy moved to Dan and said, "Dan, it's the president. Mr. Borlan wants you."

Dan picked up the phone and told the president what little he knew. He then agreed to meet the Security Council in two hours with whatever information he could gather.

As the information trickled in, all reports were similar. Blasts on main power distribution lines, all explosions took down multiple towers in a row. Repair would take time. Like the last time, all occurred in remote regions with not one casualty. As close as they could figure, around fifty locations were hit. How could this happen with no sort of lead? How could this be carried out without any Intel? Not a thread of a leak? Impossible! Completely impossible!

Dan gathered the list of targets John had handed him while Mark gave Dan his summary of the immediate impact and any long-term effects as they knew them now. Cindy did her best to compile a list of cities and regions that were affected. With all the information in hand, Dan headed off to meet with the Security Council.

Walking into the meeting, Dan could hear generators running everywhere. His heart sank thinking of all the millions that were going without power while the great county they lived in had no answers, not even the slightest clue to figure this out. As he entered the room, he could see the concern on all of the faces as he greeted the president.

Jim Borlan rose, looked at Dan and asked him to proceed. Dan walked around the room, handing each one a packet of information. Then he began. "Gentlemen and ladies. What I handed you is what little we know now. What we experienced is an attack on the United States like no other, with the exception of the attack exactly one month ago. The attack was enormous in scope and occurred simultaneously throughout the entire country, as it was on the attack last month. It appears impossible to have been carried out by one man. An army from within seems much more credible. Like what we found over the past month, no evidence on how they interact or communicate, let alone fly completely unnoticed to the government or any local law enforcement. Let me be clear. This will tear our country apart as we investigate. The nation has not gotten back on our feet after the last attack a month ago. This will cripple the country even further. The only lead I still possess is the letter. We had better start addressing the demands or figure out who and why this is happening. What we found out early on is that only the main aboveground powerlines were hit. At the locations we already have people at, it looks as though it's primary powerlines that feed heavily populated areas. The locations we have seen in the last couple of hours completely blew up huge towers that hold the powerlines, taking them to the ground. And not just one at a location. We saw eight towers outside of Washington and twelve towers taken down in Southeastern Ohio. As we are able to reach every location over the next day, I will be better able to figure the scope of the operation. I will tell you that the local power officials say it's catastrophic and will take time to repair the damage. That's all I can give you within the little time I've had."

Jim Borlan thanked Dan for the assessment. Then he looked about the room and told everyone seated, "This must be figured out! Every resource the United States has (military, federal, state and local) must cooperate to get this fixed and find who is at fault! Now gentlemen. I must address the public. Rest assured! You thought the riots because of gas were bad? This will be difficult to overcome! The people demand answers! As everyone knows, we have squat! Nothing to give! Only a promise and, as you know, that means nothing to them!"

June 17: As the sun rose in Al-Rawhen, Syria, a large group of men kneeled in prayers. As it ended, Ayatollah El Fazaza requested a group of men to meet him in his quarters.

As they assembled and scattered around the room, he rose. "I have heard reports out of the West that once again, my prince and valiant squad are bringing the infidels to their knees. The reports say much disruptions and rioting are bringing the corrupt state to its knees. As we see them falling apart, let me tell you that this is being carried out for Allah's sake. DeShawn, our greatest warrior, has brought forth this great plan and shown us the path. You are the chosen few who know our plan. Our brothers around the world know nothing. As DeShawn has shown us, it is only through vast planning and complete secrecy that this can be accomplished. With the complete success in the first two stages, it is time to set about the final stage of the plan. Each of you was handpicked and trained by DeShawn. Now those twenty-five strong left by my side will plan the next chapter. Our objective is not the United States. It will be in ruin after Stage 3. Our objective is the other havens for infidels scattered throughout Europe. Let's start the planning stage so in the new year Islam will rule the world as we see fit and as Allah would desire! Ahemd Zuhari, I have selected you to travel to the United States. I wish you to sacrifice two dear brothers who helped in planning. Their knowledge is too great to just be left unguarded. I wish Omar Kalief and Mahammed Majid to forfeit their lives for the grace of Allah. Their locations and travel arrangements are in this folder. The rest of you, please use my compound to train. You will find a map in the compound with a list of target areas, as well as the banks that keep your initial funds to get started. Let's all pray."

June 12th, 9:00 A.M.: Dan assembled his team for an update. "Okay, everyone! You have had twenty-four hours. Let's see what we got and put it all together. John, you lead off."

"Well, sir, it appears exactly fifty targets were hit, all major power-feeding powerlines. The big ones, sir, all of them, had at least eight to fourteen towers completely destroyed. The charges were set at four of the bases, completely destroying the top of the foundation, mangling the steel beyond repair. When the towers fell, the lines were snapped. They knew how to destroy them completely. The scope and planning of where and how to place the explosives without a hint of detection."

Cindy was next. "Sir, right now we have 80% of America without power. Riots went on all night in every American city. There is so much damage and casualties that no one can compile any data. Sir, it seems if you don't get a handle on this, our country will fail within days."

Dan asked Mark, "Please tell me something good."

"Well, sir, kind of," Mark said. "I have been on the phone with the power companies. They make up the Eastern Interconnection, Western Interconnection, Texas Interconnection and the Quebec Interconnection. They came up with a Band-Aid repair to get most power back on, maybe by the week's end. It doesn't build back the towers. It involves stringing new line between the good towers and burying it in concrete. The problem with it is that it puts splices in the lines, causing voltage drops. No one has had time to see what that drop will be but we can restore power to most pretty quickly. I know it sounds bizarre but the plan is already being implemented."

Dan responded, "Thank God for American ingenuity! We need the good news! Okay, guys. I know last month was a lot but let's dig deep and keep working."

Dan arrived at the Security Council for his daily meeting. Inside, all seemed extremely solemn. As he sat, Jim Borlan rose to speak.

"All this is the most historic day in the history of our great country. In one hour, I'll address our nation. Starting at 9:00 tonight and every night hereafter, I will declare Martial Law. I have met with all of the armed forces to bring all home. All active-duty members will be called into action immediately. All National Guard members will now be activated. They all will be tasked with bringing order to the nation. Several states activated their guards during the gas shortage. Crime in the last month rose 500%! Rioting, looting, murders. All rose out of control. Now, in one night, the nation was nearly torn apart. Every major city in the country was severely damaged last night. We will experience another tonight. The nation can't survive this. So for the first time, we can no longer protect anyone on foreign soil. We are in battle for the very existence of our nation. If this doesn't stop within a week, we will be reduced lower than any third-world nation. We need answers now and we need whoever is causing this found and stopped.

This is for the very existence of our country! Now I realize it's very soon into the crisis but I hope someone has some shred of good news. Who wants to be first?"

Dan rose and started, "Mr. President, as much as I would like to give you information on who's responsible, I cannot. But I do have a little something. My staff has met with the members of the four major controlling power collation of the nation: the Eastern, Western, Texas and Quebec Interconnection. The nation is interconnected by a grid of powerlines. Any power brought up at one location will trickle throughout, as long as we get continuity across the grid. The way the explosions blew up the towers, reconstructing them quickly is out of the question. As we speak, we have an army of workers and excavating equipment headed to each and every location. Our plan is to splice new lines between the destroyed sections and buy new underground wires to complete continuity to the power grid. We should start seeing power come back on within a day and a half. But saying this, with all the splices, the voltage drop on the huge wires will be great. No one knows what the strength of our power grid will be. But I will tell you to be back to full strength, it will take billions and years to get there."

The president broke in, "Great news! This is something, at least! I want the armed forces to protect these men as they go about this task. Dan, do you need help from anyone else?"

"I don't believe so, sir," Dan responded. "The escort will help as we get men and supplies to all of the locations. As you know, it's a nightmare out there."

"Okay," the president replied. "All I can say is that I hope this works. We need big things right now! Please! Someone give me a shred of information on who or whom is doing this!"

One week later, back in Roswell, DeShawn was walking into his home while off in the distance he could hear the rumblings of generators.

He had just checked on his and decided to watch the news and begin writing his next (maybe last) letter to his comrades. The news brought in the message of the explosions and the massive nationwide power outage. But what was much more forefront was the stories of the riots every city was experiencing. The pictures of cities at night only lit by the hundreds of burning buildings. They told stories of so many murders with people who could not be gathered from the streets due to the rioting. They told of the Martial Law set down by the president, along with pictures of every National Guard unit in the United States in 100% mobilization. They showed pictures of returning soldiers from overseas, as well as all of the troops in the States being activated.

He said smugly, taking all in, "How weak are they?" DeShawn thought, *Their suffering has just begun! If this doesn't send them to a point of no return, the next chapter surely will!*

With his ego firmly appeased, he started writing his letters to his comrades. In them, he spoke of the next chapter that they must complete. It would surely be the most challenging. The charges must be more precise and planned out, as well as many more targets must be set to bring about the desired outcome. He praised all for sticking with the plan. He also praised them for their conviction to remain silent, as not to tip their hats. The government hadn't a clue to who they were. The infidels would all fall.

With one week passed since the crisis, about 40% of the power was restored nationwide. But this did little to quiet the riots or stop the murderous thugs from ravaging the country. There were stories of Army units being overrun and State Capitol buildings overrun and destroyed. Washington itself was a fortress. It was protected around and within by two battalions of soldiers with all the weapons the armed forces had. Washington had one of ten airports that were open nationwide. It was packed so tightly with fighter jets and helicopters that they could barely take off.

The Security Council gathered for their daily briefing. A man with an FBI badge came rushing in.

"What are you doing?" Josh Jordan asked him.

"Sir! You have a call and you really have to take this!" he exclaimed.

"Mr. President, excuse me, please. I'm really sorry," Josh Jordan told him.

With that, the president gestured him to leave and asked the rest to continue.

In the outer office, Josh picked up the phone and he was overheard saying, "Really?! Are you kidding?!!! Get him under cover and get him to Washington NOW! Use every resource to protect him! I mean every resource!!!" With that, he hung up and rushed back into the office. "Sorry, Mr. President, but you must hear this! Our Philadelphia office got a call today from a dean at Temple University. He told my agents the story of a young, promising student that was granted a scholarship in Mechanical Engineering. His IQ was off the charts! He gave a thesis that was so disturbing the university expelled him immediately! Mr. President! The thesis that young man laid out was exactly what the terrorists are doing to the nation right now!"

The president demanded, "Let's get that man here now! I want to know everything he knows! Now, everyone, get on this NOW!"

Two hours later, a Black Hawk helicopter landed. Dean Moore stepped out and was greeted by a group of Marines. He was escorted to a Humvee and whisked off to the White House. Inside the Situation Room of the Security Council, Dean Moore laid out a story, told to him years ago. It was a story of an unfortunate young man who was passed around family to family. A story of a young man who met with many unfortunate incidents, many not of his making. So many that it landed him in juvenile penal hands until almost his 17th birthday. With all that said, the young man withstood it all to become the most learned person he had ever met. Dean Moore never quite understood why this young man would throw such a promising career out the window.

"That's it!" the president exclaimed. "I want the FBI and the CIA to look at his whole existence. Figure out where he was before the thesis. And more importantly, where he was after that. But mostly, where he is NOW!"

The next week went by with news trickling in. They traced DeShawn's passport information to where he went to Syria but then he disappeared, until he was tracked down, reappearing in GA. On the other hand, the country continued, despite the power being at 95% completely back on. Businesses, factories, and homes everywhere had been burnt to the ground. With all of the armed forces roaming the streets, they couldn't stop the equally armed citizens. If it wasn't for the gangs in the inner cities wreaking havoc, it was armed militia. In the rural areas, many had taken up building fortresses. Heavily armed guards kept everyone out, even the Army. Rumors floated about of Army personnel looting what they could find. Even cases of rape. No one trusted anyone.

Back in Georgia, DeShawn had left to do his part in the next chapter. It seemed like minutes until the FBI came in force. DeShawn's tax records led them to McNeil Enterprises. Besides having been told DeShawn was an exceptional worker, no useful information was found. However, posting him as the Most Wanted Person in the United States proved to be very useful. Hundreds of tips came pouring in, especially from Roswell. The FBI poured into the small town and immediately spread out to question everybody. Most of the businesses were boarded up. No one could be seen on the streets. But nearing the post office, they saw two armed postal workers looking out of the windows. The agents flashed their badges and the postal workers waved them in. The agents asked the two if they knew of DeShawn. They both shook their heads in acknowledgment.

The short bald-headed man spoke first. "That's an odd fellow, for sure! He's probably the only fellow left that actually writes letters by hand. And not just one or two, lots and lots, going to all over the country. Not only that, but he gets them back. He claimed they were in some kind of college fraternity or something like that. But for our only darkie in town, he was nice. Paid cash for everything. Don't even know if he had a cell phone or a credit card. Very odd, indeed."

"Do you know where he lives?" the agent asked.

"Of course!" the postal workers said. "We know where everyone lives. He lives back at Paul McNaire's old place. 'Bout a mile from here. We can take you if you want. No mail today so nothing to do."

"You spoke of letters to everywhere. Do you recall where?" the agent asked.

"Well, sir, not exactly, but I do remember sorting the letter. It seemed to me that they went to every region in the States. I recall some in California, New York, Oregon, Florida, Texas, Oklahoma and a lot more. I recall them being very scattered. No one grouping. Just scattered."

"Thanks for your help," the agent replied. "That's very useful. Now if you don't mind, sir, I believe we would like to see where this gentleman calls home."

As they approached the driveway, the agent told the postal workers to return to their office. "We don't know what to expect."

Stopping before they traveled down the driveway, they made a call to Josh Jordan to seek instructions. Josh instructed them to surround the property and to stay out of sight until they knew he was there. He told them not to park in the driveway. If he was inside, they needed to get him alive. If he wasn't, they needed to lure him into their trap. But under no circumstances was he to be harmed.

The agents fanned out and began watching. No sign of DeShawn was found. After the next morning, they decided to send in a squad to scout around. Still no sign of him. With it being July 4th, the agents settled in. This was their best hope of catching him. Their only lead.

Back in Washington, the Security Council had assembled. Today there was much news.

Josh started off, "Well, Mr. President, we have pieced together what we think is the nearest scenario from the information collected in Roswell. To the best of our knowledge, DeShawn is a leader of sleepers planted all over the country. The reason there was no chatter is that they didn't communicate that way. They went old school. They sent letters."

"Letters?" the president asked.

"Yes, sir," Josh replied. "From what the postal workers said, maybe twenty to thirty locations. No records were kept on the addresses. But what's for sure is that this is like no terrorist operation we have ever seen. There was no way to see this coming. There was no way to stop it. After two months, this is what information we have."

The president spoke up, "We need him alive at all costs!"

Everyone agreed.

"We have one week, gentlemen, to find him and stop the next attack! If our nation isn't already doomed, one more will seal the deal! Let's keep digging! It's for our very existence!"

At the farm, there was still no sign of DeShawn for the next few days. Then suddenly, during the night of July 8th, a Toyota pickup pulled down the driveway. A black man matching DeShawn's description got out of the truck. He walked behind it to an outbuilding and fired up a generator. The lights in the house lit up and he went inside. Shortly thereafter, most went out. It appeared that he went to bed. The agents decided to wait until daylight to confront him.

Daylight came. The agents closed in to make the chance of escape less likely. When they spotted DeShawn moving around, they brought out a bullhorn.

"DeShawn! Your house is surrounded! Come out peacefully and you won't be harmed! We just want to talk!"

To their amazement, he immediately walked out on the porch with his hands over his head. "Look!" DeShawn exclaimed. "I'm not armed," he said as he spun in a circle. "You have me! No problem!" He walked down the first step.

"Stop right there!" the agent yelled.

DeShawn exclaimed, "It's okay! I'll go willingly! No fight!"

As DeShawn stepped off the last step and onto the ground, the agents couldn't see the implanted detonator at ground level. With the last step, a massive explosion occurred! It leveled the house, barn and all of the outbuildings. DeShawn and any of the agents close to the building were killed instantly!

The morning of July 11th, back in Washington, the Security Counsel was gathered at 8:30 A.M.

Jim stood and told the group, "This is very grave. We cut the head off of the snake but got nothing to show for it! The country is in ruins! We are running a shell of a government! Most states don't even have any infrastructure. We are what little is left! Let's pray nothing else happens as we wait for the 9-o'clock hour!"

When 9:00 came, no phone calls came in about explosions. Nothing. At 9:02, they all noticed there was no cell signal. Nothing! Everyone lost all Internet! They were blind to what just happened!

EPILOGUE

May 9, 2032: The Heads of Security in England, France, Spain and Germany strolled into their respective offices. As they each strolled in, each as usual opened their emails. As each opened their messages, they all discovered a very unusual message with the heading "Of National Importance." The message read: "Today marks the 5th anniversary of the letter sent to the United States that set forth a string of events that brought the once great nation to its ruins. Today, you receive the same message. By now, you know it was the Islamic people who brought about the destruction of the United States. It is now our desire that your nations suffer the same fate. At 9:00 A.M. on May 11th, your nations will go down the same path of destruction! Praise Allah! May the Islamic people rise to never encountered heights!"